Light
— IN THE —
DARKNESS

By:

Samika Collins

Published By Onney Publishing & Performances, Inc.

Publishing
Editing
Book Cover Design By:
Onney Publishing & Performances, Inc.
Missouri City, Texas 77459
www.onney.net

ABOUT THE AUTHOR

Samika Collins has lived in Texas all her life. She enjoys reading and writing. She has used her writing skills throughout her career with *Light in the Darkness* being her first published book. She gives all glory to God. She also enjoys home design, watching professional and college football, going bowling, comedy shows and plays. She is dedicated to her family and friends. She is the mother to one son and grandmother to one grandson. She has been gifted in her life with relationships that exemplifies the love of God. Her greatest joy is being able to be a blessing to others. Being able to work alongside her partner in life in ministry has blessed her and given her life new meaning and purpose.

PROLOGUE

As she entered the turnstiles of DDV Abyss Inc., she walked into darkness. As she moved, she thought the light would automatically switch on. There was nothing, so she stood still. She allowed her eyes to adjust to the dark, but all she saw was darkness. She listened to hear for anything that would lead her to light, but she heard nothing. She felt around on the walls for a light switch, but she found none. She finally pulled out her cell phone and cut on her flashlight. What Camtrelle saw, heard, and felt would change her forever. As she continued to walk down the aisles, Camtrelle came to realize she was being initiated into an atmosphere of pure darkness. The darkness was the lying, the adultery, the fornication, the stealing, the mental and physical abuse, the drugs and alcohol, the pessimism, and the lack of trust and integrity. The darkness that would consume her.

The people she worked with would become her life and family. Her mornings, days, nights, weekends, and holidays would be spent with her work family. Camtrelle started out with a strong commitment to her family, friends, place of worship, and other activities, but as the years progressed in the system, her resolve to stay strong to her commitments weakened, little by little, over time, until she could no longer distinguish herself from the darkness. The light that once shone brightly within her became dimmer and dimmer until it finally went out and she was no longer there. She would become someone that she did not recognize, did not know, and did not respect. The darkness that she felt, she wanted others to feel, so she would slowly bring others into the darkness, one by one, until the only light came from cell phones and computer screens. Everyone within the walls of DDV Abyss Inc. became infected with the darkness to a certain extent. It all began with signing the confidentiality agreement.

TABLE OF CONTENTS

PART I: ENTERING THE DARKNESS

Camtrelle met the boy she was going to marry in the third grade. He was the cutest little boy she had ever seen. His name was Josiah. He was so shy and had this awkward walk. He was friends with her next-door neighbor Kendrick. One day he found the nerve to ask her if he could walk her home. He would walk with Kendrick while Camtrelle would walk with her friends. Camtrelle's grandmother was very mean and somewhat strict, so Camtrelle would talk to Josiah across the fence while he was at Kendrick's house. Every now and then, Camtrelle's grandmother would allow Josiah to visit, and they would sit on the porch. Camtrelle was so shy around him. She could never look at him while he was looking at her. Every chance she got she would take quick glances at him when he was not paying attention. Josiah walking Camtrelle home went on throughout the rest of elementary school. He even got into a fight to defend her. A boy named Tremaine was always bullying her; Josiah wanted to protect her from him and wanted him to leave her alone. Camtrelle did not see the fight, but she heard about it.

Tremaine eventually left her alone. The end of elementary was difficult because Josiah and Camtrelle knew they would be going to two different middle schools. They exchanged phone numbers to keep in touch and keep the friendship going. It worked for a while, but things became more difficult. Camtrelle was always at worship service and did not have the time to talk to Josiah. She was there all-day Sunday (10:00 service, 3:00 service, 7:00 service), drill team practice on Monday, bible study on Wednesday, choir rehearsal on Thursday, and anything that may happen in between. Camtrelle loved going to worship service and being involved in the different activities. She was able to establish a firm foundation in her relationship with God.

Meanwhile, Josiah was doing his thing. He was involved in a lot of sport activities and the drama team. They just did not have the time to talk to one another, so they grew apart. They would speak occasionally just to stay in touch. When Camtrelle got into high school and was able to drive, she made a beeline to see Josiah. She knew where he lived and not only kept in touch with him, but also his mom did not work too far from where Camtrelle lived. Camtrelle did not just pop up at his house. Josiah knew she was coming. Camtrelle was going to make sure she looked good for Josiah. She wore a red mini skirt with a black sweater. She was old school, so she had on a pair of stockings with some black low heel pumps. Her red frame eyeglasses matched the outfit perfectly. Camtrelle wore a little bit of makeup to enhance her looks and her hair was styled short. When Josiah saw Camtrelle, his eyes lit up. He complimented her and invited her into his home.

They sat down and talked and caught up on each other's lives. Camtrelle was leaving and she gave Josiah a hug. Next thing you know, Josiah and Camtrelle's lips met, and they experienced their first kiss. Camtrelle thought this may be the beginning of them getting together and being in a relationship. She came to see him on several other occasions, but Camtrelle did not feel that vibe from him that he wanted the same thing, so she backed off. Life went on for Camtrelle and Josiah. She had met this guy at a friend's party. She had heard a lot about him. All the girls wanted him. When he would come on campus, all the girls would make sure their hair was in place and their makeup was on point. They wanted his attention. Camtrelle was trying to figure out what was the big deal. He looked nice and had a nice build but nothing to lose your mind over. To say that Camtrelle was shocked when he expressed interest in her was an understatement. From the night of the party, Camtrelle and Jeremy were inseparable. They were together all the time. Jeremy was older than Camtrelle, so he was out of school while she still had two years left. She was a good student and stayed focused on her studies.

The lessons and assignments came easy to Camtrelle. She was able to remember things without really studying. When she graduated, she always knew she wanted to go to college, but she was so burnt out on all the schoolwork. She really did not think about where she wanted to go. After talking with her friend, Camtrelle made the different decision. Camtrelle and Jeremy knew this time was coming. Camtrelle wanted things in life and wanted to be successful, however, she defined success in her mind. Jeremy had not done anything to better himself. When Camtrelle went off to school, the first thing she did was join the school choir and find a worship center.

She had a part-time job at home and transferred locations when she went to school. Jeremy would come visit from time to time, and Camtrelle would drive back home to see him. Camtrelle was getting increasingly frustrated with Jeremy because he still was not doing anything with his life. He kept saying he was going to do something, but there was no action. Camtrelle had finally had enough. and the relationship ended. Jeremy was hurt by Camtrelle's decision. He tried to get back with Camtrelle. He moved to where Camtrelle was going to school and got a job, but for Camtrelle, it was too late. She found herself interested in the pastor's son at the worship center she was attending. They had become friends and would talk on the phone from time to time and sometimes hang out. She met his family and would visit him at his home. He would also come by her place. Jeremy learned about him and felt that was why he was not given the chance to be with Camtrelle again.

Jeremy gave up on Camtrelle and moved back home, but things were not over with Camtrelle. She would come home and be with Jeremy as if they were still together. During one of those times is when she was gifted with her son. One night while working her part-time job, Camtrelle saw a coworker that reminded her of Josiah. This was her first time seeing him. Seeing this guy made Camtrelle reach out to Josiah's mom. Her number was always the same. While talking to her, Camtrelle found out that Josiah was married. For some reason, Camtrelle felt the need to ask was Josiah happy. There was silence on the other end. This gave Camtrelle her answer. Josiah's mom let him know that she called and asked about him. A few days later, Josiah called Camtrelle, and it was as if there had not been years since the last time they had spoken.

The Initiation

Camtrelle was at a point in her life where she did not know what she wanted to do with her life. Things did not turn out according to her plans. She had her life all mapped out in her head. She was a smart girl that did well in school. She was going to go to college, get her degree as an anesthesiologist, marry the love of her life, have two kids, live in her dream house which she already designed in her mind, and drive her beamer. Life took a turn for her when she went off to college. While at school, she got sick with a sinus infection. She went to the school clinic for medication and had an allergic reaction to the medication. At the same time, she found out she was pregnant by her ex, Jeremy. Camtrelle cried because she was disappointed in herself. She felt like she let down her mom and grandpa.

She was fearful of telling her mom the news; her grandpa had already gone to be with the Lord. Camtrelle made the phone call to her mom, and she took the news better than Camtrelle thought she would. The child's father, not so much. He said he did not think baby was his. Jeremy thought the baby belonged to the pastor's son. Camtrelle told him she never had sex with him. She liked him, but they were only good friends. Actually, he was intimidated by Camtrelle because he felt she was experienced. He did not think he would be able to please her. He was the first guy that Camtrelle knew that openly admitted to having a small penis. Camtrelle never found out if that was true. She was only with Jeremy. Days had passed, and Camtrelle was still having effects from the allergic reaction.

It had progressively gotten worse to where her hands were in so much pain that she could barely use them. Camtrelle knew she could no longer remain at school. She had to go back home. She withdrew from school, and her brother Waylenn along with his wife Chrysann packed up her belongings and took Camtrelle home. Camtrelle continued to get worse until she could barely walk. It came to a point where she was using a cane and a wheelchair because of all the pain in her feet. She cried all day and all night because of the pain. Being pregnant, she really could not take medication. It would possibly put her baby at risk of birth defects. Jeremy tried to comfort her, but nothing he did helped. Camtrelle went to all kinds of specialists to get a diagnosis, but to no avail. To this day, Camtrelle never knew what was happening with her body during that time. With the miraculous, manifesting healing power of Jehovah Rapha, Camtrelle was made whole.

Camtrelle was signing the confidentiality agreement. She had taken an exam for DDV Abyss Inc. for several positions months before, but really did not think anything more about it. She was content with her job as a teacher's aide for the school district. She made enough money to take care of her lifestyle and her baby. The first time she received a letter from the company offering her a position, she declined. She did not respond to the letter. Her brother Waylenn, already working at the company, tried to convince her why she should work at the service company. She listened to him and gave it some thought. The next time she received a letter from the company, she responded and decided to take the job offer. She turned in her two weeks' notice to the district and prepared herself for this new chapter in her life.

When Camtrelle signed that statement, she had no idea what she was doing. What was she vowing or pledging to do or who was she vowing or pledging to? In that orientation, Camtrelle received her work assignment. The group she started with were all assigned to the third shift. They all looked around at one another because it was going to be a big change in their lives. They were called flex employees. They were not even full-time employees whereas many of them had left full time jobs. When they were scheduled to work, they were only guaranteed four hours per day. They did not have to be scheduled. There was so much uncertainty. Camtrelle knew that many of them wanted to run back to their old jobs, but they had already resigned. None of them really knew how things operated within the company, so the union was able to put the fear in them to join.

Management put the fear in them that they would be fired while on probation if they were late or missed a day. They were also informed after signing the agreement that they would be required to work every weekend and holiday. Camtrelle wondered what in the world had she gotten herself into. Camtrelle and many of the people she started with reported for duty the first night an hour early. They were afraid to be late. They waited at the time clock for thirty minutes before they could clock in because they did not want to clock in late. Their supervisor, Cinna Minson, gave them assignments and paired them with regular employees for training. Their breaks and lunch were 15 and 30 minutes, respectively. When taking her first break, Camtrelle heard some of the guys saying, "new meat". She did not know the meaning of what they were saying, so she asked one of the guys that was not a part of the group. "New meat" was a fresh group of females that was just starting that they would attempt to have sex with. Camtrelle was always like one of the guys, so it did not phase her.

She knew nothing was going to go down. She had her man Josiah at home, and although they were having problems, he was her future. She was focused on her new job and fixing her relationship. Camtrelle must admit that there was this one guy that piqued her interest, Liam. Every time she would go by his machine to sweep the mail, he would say what he would do to her. He would tell Camtrelle that he would have her crawling up the bed trying to get away from him because he would be pleasuring her so good. He would describe his curved penis and say how sex is different with a guy that has a curved penis. Liam described his penis as being curved like a banana. Well, Camtrelle had never seen or heard of a penis being curved like a banana, so she was a little curious, but not curious enough to jeopardize her already rocky relationship. Camtrelle had been unfaithful before, so she was trying to do everything she could to rebuild the trust in her relationship. Liam and Camtrelle became good friends as the years went on but never crossed that line. Camtrelle can say that Liam had a good record in having the women take off their panties.

The Invitation

As the days went on, Camtrelle watched the guys continue their attempts with the women. It took them awhile, but they continued until it was time for the next step into the initiation. It began with "Let's go to breakfast". Once they got you outside of the workplace, it was a done deal. Camtrelle was not having any of it. Her focus was on Josiah, but things were going downhill with him fast. He could not get past her infidelity. It was not the physical act that he could not get past, but the fact that she blamed him for the reason she did it. She did not want to take responsibility for her own actions and decisions. The sex meant nothing to Camtrelle; neither did the guy. It was like an out-of-body experience for her. Her body was there and that was the only thing that was there. In Camtrelle's mind, Wyatt was fulfilling a need that she had.

You see, Camtrelle had self-esteem and daddy issues, so she was searching for attention from whomever would give it to her. Wyatt gave her that attention, so she gave him what he wanted. Josiah was not able to give her the attention she was longing for. Not being able to come to an understanding drove them further apart. Josiah had become mean and verbally abusive. One night when they were out, they got into an argument, and Camtrelle had decided she had enough. She asked him for her key back and then drove off. She felt that some space between them was needed. What a mistake that was. Meanwhile at work, everything was going good for Camtrelle. She was working 6 days a week up to 12 hours a day. The money was good, although much of her life was given to make it. She had made some friends with the group that she started with, and they would all go to breakfast as a group.

Then it happened. Camtrelle was asked out to breakfast. Not by just anyone, but by her married boss. Mr. Sealy was a pervert. He would leer at all the women as if he was undressing them. You could feel his eyes on you, even when your back was to him. Camtrelle did not even know how he felt comfortable asking her to go anywhere with him. She had limited conversations with him. When he asked Camtrelle out, he had a receipt in his hand that showed a $7K balance, and he grabbed her hand with his other hand. It was such an unnatural and disgusting feeling.

Camtrelle politely turned him down and then went to the restroom and scrubbed her hand. Something in how he was holding her hand just did not feel right, and Camtrelle was trying to wash that feeling away. Eventually, Mr. Sealy got himself into some trouble for his lewd behavior. The only thing that happened to him was that he was moved to another work area. Now he could have the same behavior with another group of employees. There was no serious consequence for sexual harassment. Management would take a training course, the employees would take a training course, and the sexual harassment would continue. Camtrelle got a new boss who was trouble with a capital T and things went on as usual. Camtrelle and her group of friends continued going to breakfast and having a good time.

Camtrelle's new boss Kristen Dickinson had it going on and she knew it. When she walked into the room, everyone was going to notice her. She had a shape that all the men drooled over and all the women wished they had. She had a walk that went along with her figure. She would sway her hips, toss her long hair, give you a look with her piercing dark eyes, then give you a smile that says, I know you want to be like me. Her look was all hers, au natural. Although she could probably have any man she wanted, she only wanted one, Drew. Drew was tall, dark, and dripping with masculinity and male sexiness. It was rumored that he was packing the ultimate package. This not only came from women, but from men also, who were not in any type of way gay, but may have caught a glimpse in the men's room while relieving themselves.

Drew was married, but that did not stop him from sleeping with the women that he wanted to be with. Kristen was crazy about him and determined to have him. Drew and Kristen eventually became a couple while he was still married. She would be at work hanging out with him instead of managing her unit. One time Drew and Kristen were in the ladies' locker room talking. Many of the female employees had been in and out of the locker room and had seen them in there. One of them went and reported them to her boss. Kristen was called to the office and came back to the unit pissed. She called Camtrelle to the office to see if she reported her, like she would say she did even *if* she did, but she had not. She then proceeded to call everyone else, one by one, to the office asking them the same thing like they were going to tell her anything. She never did find out who reported her. She started being mean towards her employees because she felt she could not trust them.

Camtrelle and her friends continue to perform their jobs and were not concerned about Ms. Dickinson having an attitude with them. She eventually moved on to another job, and

Camtrelle was starting to see that that this was just how the company operated.

The Intention

Camtrelle decided enough time had passed between her and Josiah, so she reached out to him. It was so good to hear his voice. Camtrelle had never given up on them. In her mind, her future was with him. At the time, Camtrelle and her son had been living at home. She used that opportunity to buy things for her new place, so she would only have to pay the rent and not have a lot of other bills. She got a storage facility for all the things she was purchasing. She told Josiah about her plans to eventually move out, but she wanted to be a little more financially stable. Unbeknownst to Camtrelle, Josiah had moved on with his life. He had been communicating with an ex and they were in a relationship. He had moved to some apartments in the southwest part of the city. Once Camtrelle was able to move on her own, she moved into some apartments across the street from where Josiah was living. Josiah told Camtrelle that they were only roommates. He even brought her over to their place. Josiah would come to Camtrelle's place, spend time with her and even spend the night. Then he would go back home. Well, it was not enough for Camtrelle. She did not understand why he was not leaving his roommate and moving in with her since he claimed to love Camtrelle and wanted to be with her. Something was not adding up.

Meanwhile, Camtrelle started to change. She was tired of being by herself, and she thought she deserved better than what she was getting from Josiah. Camtrelle went shopping and she bought jeans, tops, and new shoes that would make her feel good about herself. She bought new underwear and bras to make her feel sexy and it worked. She felt eyes on her when she walked in the breakroom. The attention felt good to her. She did not want any of the guys, just a little of the attention. Camtrelle and her friends had started to work in other areas when they were short-staffed. Camtrelle started to work a lot with this guy named Vance. Vance was quiet and to himself. He would go on break and lunch by himself instead of hanging out with his coworkers.

Camtrelle and Vance started to talk more and got to know one another as she worked more with him. There was a little spark between them but no fireworks. They exchanged numbers and started talking on the phone. Camtrelle started spending more time talking to Vance than Josiah. Josiah picked up on something being different with Camtrelle. Camtrelle finally confronted Josiah about his living situation. He finally broke down and told her truth; he was married. Camtrelle remained strong in front of Josiah, but she was devastated. Her heart had been broken into so many pieces that she vowed she would not let that happen again. In her heart and mind, she and Josiah were over for good, for life. Not only was the relationship over, but the friendship as well. Josiah and Camtrelle had been friends since the third grade. He knew her better than anyone. Now all of that was lost. Camtrelle did not want to dwell on the hurt and pain that she was feeling, so she turned all her attention to Vance.

Vance and Camtrelle really started feeling one another as they continued to get to know one another. They would hang out together on break and just talk. Finally, they decided to go out. Once you go outside of the workplace, they got you. Since they both worked nights, they had a lunch date. They went out for Mexican food and drinks. Camtrelle enjoyed his company. Over the course of several months, they went out a few more times. The first time they kissed one another was at work in the locker room. Vance was a great kisser. Camtrelle often thought that they could be participants in a Big Red commercial. There came a point in their unestablished relationship when they thought it was time to take things to the next level. They made arrangements for him to come over to Camtrelle's place. When he arrived, they both knew why he was there. Things did not go according to plan. The situation was extremely awkward. Talk about incompatibility. Vance left before it was time for her to pick her child up from school. Nothing changed between them, even after that mishap. Actually, it got better.

Vance invited Camtrelle to a family reunion out of town. Camtrelle was excited. A trip out of town and meeting the family. Camtrelle thought this was big. Thought it meant something. Camtrelle went on the trip, and it had its highs and lows. Camtrelle met some of the family but not the main family; his parents and sister did not attend. She was introduced to aunts, uncles, and a few cousins which did not go well. One of his cousins felt like Camtrelle wanted her husband. Camtrelle was not thinking about her husband. Her husband sat next to Camtrelle on the sofa, and they were laughing and talking. The cousin did not like it. She was right there in the room with them the entire time. At the end of the day, she did apologize for her behavior. They were going through some things at the time. Camtrelle was very understanding. Later that night in the hotel room, Camtrelle and Vance were talking.

He was telling her that he really did feel like they were incompatible when it came to sex. Camtrelle was good with it. She went and took a shower and got ready for bed. It seems that Vance wanted to make sure his theory was right, so he started caressing Camtrelle. She responded and one thing led to another.

That was the first time they were together. Camtrelle and Vance continued to see one another. She would go visit him at his place, hang out at work, and take day trips. Camtrelle could see a possible future with him. She was not in love and never said she loved him, but she could grow to love him. While Camtrelle was thinking about a future with Vance, he was putting on the brakes. He started having an attitude with her, talking to her less, not wanting to see her at work. Camtrelle did not know what caused the sudden change.

She thought things were going well and felt like she was in a relationship, although there was never a conversation between them saying that they were. A few weeks later, he told Camtrelle what was up. He was indeed in a relationship, with someone else. Camtrelle was like how and when did this happen. Of course, he felt he did not owe her an explanation since they were not in a relationship. It was friends with benefits. Camtrelle played it cool. She let herself get caught up. Camtrelle vowed that she was not going to let that happen again. Camtrelle respected Vance and his relationship. He eventually got married. The marriage did not last. They would talk from time to time after the marriage was over. One day they started talking about God. Camtrelle invited him to visit the place where she attended service, and he did. He found a place of worship of his own that he liked, so he decided to become a member. Camtrelle gave him some material on salvation, and they talked about it until he got a clear understanding. He received salvation and was also baptized. He continued going to service and learning more of the word. Camtrelle liked to think that something good did come out of the two of them knowing one another.

The Submission

Camtrelle was once again alone where she had no choice but to listen to the voices in her head. She no longer had Vance to distract her from the pain she was feeling from losing Josiah. The pain cut her to the core. She felt so betrayed by Josiah. Camtrelle thought she was his ride or die. She had been there for him at one of the lowest points in his life. She had put her life on the line to help him. It could have cost her everything, including her baby. That is how much she loved him. When Josiah called her for help, she did not hesitate to be there for him. She gave him a safe haven, a place of refuge. Considering all that Camtrelle had done for him, she could not understand why he could not forgive her and was able to marry someone else when they had always planned to be together. Camtrelle thought he might have slept with someone else but getting married never entered her mind.

It was too much for her to handle. What made it even worse for Camtrelle is that Josiah and his wife Cassie moved into the same apartment complex where she lived. Camtrelle lived at the entrance of the complex so everyday she watched her, him, or them together pass by her place. It was a constant reminder to Camtrelle of Josiah's decision to choose someone else. Camtrelle spiraled out of control. She was going to numb the pain no matter what it took. She figured the only way to numb the pain was to find another distraction, another man. She really did not go anywhere, so the only place to meet someone was at work; her mindset was next man up.

Camtrelle had a favorite pair of jeans that she liked to wear, a light blue pair of Guess jeans. She thought they showed her off her curves. One day she saw Trenton eyeing her. She gave him a look that said I notice you noticing me, and I do not have a problem with it. From that day forward, they would give each other one of those flirtatious looks with their eyes then smile. Little by little, he would pass by her and make a comment that would make Camtrelle laugh. Camtrelle already knew about Trenton because he had already been with other women around the job. Camtrelle knew some of the women but did not care. She made her move. She looked up his number and gave him a call. Camtrelle could be bold when she wanted to be. Trenton had a girlfriend at the time that also worked at the company, but Camtrelle did not care.

She enjoyed the attention from Trenton and wanted more. Trenton was average height, wore contacts, and was a tad bit older than Camtrelle. He was nothing to write home about, but it was evident by his past that he could pull the ladies. Camtrelle and Trenton would talk on the phone getting to know one another. A few coworkers could see a difference in how they interacted. There was no more denying the attraction. He did not treat Camtrelle any differently than anyone else. She was expected to do her job and follow any instructions that were given. The phone conversations went on for a while before he asked Camtrelle to visit her place. She allowed him to come over, but nothing happened. Trenton might have been expecting something to happen, but Camtrelle was not ready to have sex with him. She was enjoying the attention and wanted it to last. She knew eventually she would have to put up or shut up, but she was going to drag it out as long as she could. When she did give in, it was like the situation with Vance.

It just was not working. Deep inside, Camtrelle knew what she was doing was wrong and that was probably the reason she was having a hard time being with him. If something did happen, it was not enjoyable for her because she could not remember it. Camtrelle was certain that he could not have enjoyed himself either. The only thing that Camtrelle can remember is that he wanted to have anal sex. Oh, that was not happening. She was wondering if the other women he had been with that she knew about had anal sex with him. To each her own, but Camtrelle was not down with no anal sex. What has to exit is bad enough, so there definitely was not any entering. Knowing he liked to have anal sex was a turn off for Camtrelle. She could not look at him the same.

He must have had many first experiences with anal sex because he was saying everything possible that would make it not hurt. Get a pillow, lay on your stomach, get some Vaseline. Nope, not happening. This was just another experience Camtrelle wanted to bury and forget ever happened. Things between Camtrelle and Trenton were not the same after that experience. The attraction was still there, and the flirting was still there but that is where it stopped. Trenton got a new position in a different department and married his girlfriend. That was the end to that fling.

****

Camtrelle had met Dixie in orientation, and they had become good friends. Dixie and Camtrelle were alike in many ways. She was able to take Camtrelle out of her comfort zone. There was a bowling team made up of the company's employees. They would host parties and Dixie always wanted to go the parties. Dixie was her girl so Camtrelle would go the parties with her. Dixie and Camtrelle would get dressed up, make sure their makeup was good, hair was on point, and then show up a little late. Camtrelle did not drink or dance, but she still had a good time. Dixie liked to drink and dance, so she always had a good time. She was very flirtatious like Camtrelle. It was always fun seeing coworkers outside of the job in a different element. They were dressed up, so they looked different than they did in their work clothes.

Sometimes coworkers would bring their spouse or girlfriend in which many times you did not know some of them were married. They never mentioned having spouses, and their behavior was definitely that of someone that was single. They were on their best behavior at those parties. When Camtrelle went to the parties, she did not go with the intent to meet anyone. She was only there in support of Dixie. Camtrelle would have conversations with some of the fellows, but that was the extent of it. Dixie, on the other hand, had a potential friend at the time so she was spending a lot of time with him. Eventually, it became a 'friends with benefits' type of situation which Dixie was used to having.

It was one commonality between the two friends. Now these parties were hosted on Saturday nights, so they had to request to be off if they wanted to go because they were scheduled to work every weekend. On some Saturday mornings, there was another club employees would go to, The Chasm. When you work the graveyard shift, the morning is your night. Of course, Dixie wanted to go. When they got off work, they would go and hang out for several hours. Other coworkers who had just worked all night would be there as well. There was food, dancing, drinks, and light conversations. Camtrelle and Dixie just sat around joking and laughing with their fellow coworkers. It was all in fun.

****

Camtrelle laid her eyes on a new prospect that piqued her interest. Now dude was fine. Had a beautiful smile. He was married, which was a good thing for Camtrelle. He would not get caught up and neither would she. Camtrelle would always speak to him, but now she started talking to him a tad bit more. One thing that Caleb did was smoke. Camtrelle had never been with anyone that smoked. She was able to look past that bad habit. Caleb would go outside on his break so he could smoke, so Camtrelle started going to the same area on her break. She did this for a while, and as she continued to go on break in the smoke area, they started talking more and more. Eventually, they exchanged numbers. Camtrelle was repeating the same pattern, making the same mistake, and at the time, she did not care. She did not care that she was hurting others knowingly and unknowingly, including herself. She knew what she was doing was wrong. Camtrelle even felt bad at times about what she was doing, but she did not let it stop her. She knew that the wages of sin were death. She knew she was giving in to a generational curse.

The women in her family committed the same sins and had that pattern of being with someone else's man. Camtrelle never thought she would be that person that lived in that iniquity. The first time she had sex with a married man, she cried until there were no more tears left. She knew at that time the generational curse had made its way to her. Throughout the short time she had been at DDV Abyss exhibiting a destructive behavior, she was going to worship service. There were ministries she would watch on television. She listened to her gospel music daily. She prayed and thanked God for her blessings. Camtrelle knew what she was sowing, she would one day reap. She knew she was in her flesh and no good thing would come from it.

Camtrelle and Caleb talked on the phone for a while before he started coming over to her place to visit. When they would get off work, he would come to her place and hang out. They would talk, watch some television, and Caleb would try to make a move. Camtrelle would put him off. She was not trying to have sex with him. She just enjoyed his company. Caleb was getting extremely frustrated with Camtrelle. He felt like she was just teasing him and leading him on. Camtrelle was not ready to let him go, but she was not ready to sleep with him either. Then one day Caleb experienced a terrible loss in his life. Camtrelle did not know how to comfort him. In her want to help him, she gave in to him. Once it was over, she felt bad about what she had done. Camtrelle knew in her mind that it would not happen again. Camtrelle and Caleb both backed away from each other after that happened. He may have felt bad as well about what occurred, although Camtrelle didn't think that it was his first time stepping out. It may have been the timing because of his loss. He did step out again, and everyone at work knew it. He and his new friend did not try to hide it. They were together for quite some time. Camtrelle did not care who he was with or what he was doing. She had her focus on things that were happening in her own life.

Camtrelle did not want to keep making the same mistakes. She knew changes had to be made in her life. Her lifestyle was a danger to her health. Her decisions were not bringing her any fulfillment, joy, or happiness. If anything, they did just the opposite. Camtrelle felt worse about herself. She wanted to do better, needed to do better. She wanted to go from being bitter to better. Camtrelle decided it was time to stop masking her pain. She was going to focus on her son and forget about men. For Camtrelle, the sex was meaningless and what she thought she was getting from the men was a false positive. She did not get anything out of it and the men probably did not either. Camtrelle was just another woman they slept with. Camtrelle did learn some things about herself through her experiences. She learned the type of person she did not want to be. She learned the type of physical connection she wanted to experience. The type of mental and emotional connection she wanted to have when she entered into a relationship. Camtrelle learned that she was not as strong as she wanted others to believe. Camtrelle wanted to become the person that she felt she was inside and only the power of God would be able to change her into that person.

Camtrelle knew that she was the light. Her light had shown brightly before, and she wanted it to shine again. She had entered into a dark place within herself, then she entered the dark atmosphere of her workplace. There were very few outlets to plug into within the facility to get power to get some light to shine. Every now and then, there were flickers of light. Camtrelle would hear or see something positive. Someone would speak truth. Others would talk about the word, their faith, and beliefs. There would be people whose light was bright, then would go dim. They had started giving into the darkness until their light was gone out. Camtrelle kept holding on to hope. She knew she had to get to the power source for her light to shine again. Until Camtrelle was willing to do what she needed to get to the source, she would adjust to the darkness.

PART II: Adapting to the Darkness

Camtrelle started having physical problems. She did not know what was going on, but all her joints were causing her pain. The pain was constant. It was affecting her home and work life. She began to miss work because she could no longer perform her duties. You name a part of her body, and it was causing discomfort. Camtrelle could not even sleep. There was no position that she could find that was comfortable. When at work, Camtrelle had a challenging time standing on her feet for extended periods and other duties she had to perform. She was afraid she might lose her job. She would come to work and could not stay the entire time. One day a friend at work told her it might be lupus based on her symptoms.

Camtrelle went to the internet and did research on lupus, and the symptoms mirrored that of lupus. She made an appointment with a doctor that did not have any available appointments for months ahead. She made an appointment with another doctor, and the circumstance was the same where there were no available appointments for months. It was whoever Camtrelle would be able to see first. She was anxious for a diagnosis and medication that would help with the pain. One doctor was across town from where she lived. She drove across town, filled out the paperwork, did bloodwork, spoke with the doctor, and then waited for the results. This was not the doctor for Camtrelle. She went back to the doctor's office when the results came back, and the doctor never gave her the results of the tests or prescribed her anything.

When she met with him, all he asked was why do you think you have lupus? Worst experience with a "professional" doctor. The experience with that doctor really ticked off Camtrelle because she still did not have answers. She was finally able to see the other doctor. She went through the same process, but this time she received an answer. It was lupus based on the test results. Camtrelle was prescribed medications to help with the symptoms and the pain, and she was given a follow up appointment. So began Camtrelle's journey with lupus.

Camtrelle gave her mother the news, and her mother began to cry. Camtrelle hugged her and assured her that she would be fine. Because Camtrelle had already been through a similar health challenge, she already knew how to fight. The devil is a liar, and Camtrelle was not claiming that she had lupus. Whose report was she going to believe? She was going to do her part in the natural while she relied on God to perform the supernatural. Camtrelle knew that every name must bow at the name of Jesus and lupus was going to bow out of her life. The same year, her friend also invited her to visit her worship place. The first time Camtrelle visited, she joined. She had already been watching this pastor on television, but it never crossed her mind to visit his place of worship. She had been a member of her ministry since she started going to worship service as a young child. It was time for a change.

It was time for growth. Camtrelle was learning so much more at this new service. She was attending bible study and all the special services and events that were going on at the worship center. She focused on her health and building her relationship with God. She had her good days and bad days when it came to her health. The medications helped and she could manage the pain. Her attendance improved and she was able to perform her duties once again at a productive level. During this time, she was not messing around with anyone. Camtrelle had reached a point where she no longer wanted to continue in those destructive behaviors. She asked God to forgive her for the things she had done that she knew was wrong, the sins she committed knowingly and the things she did that were wrong unknowingly. God forgave her, but the hardest part was forgiving herself. The devil always reminded her of the things she did in her past. She needed to release the guilt and shame.

Camtrelle understood that her past mistakes did not define her. She did not allow the judgement and condemnation of others to keep her head down. For all have sinned and fallen short of the glory of God. None of us live in glass houses. Who without sin can cast the first stone? Jesus was the only person to walk this earth without sin. As Camtrelle was growing in the knowledge of God, she was growing in the knowledge of who she was in Christ.

The Adaptation

Camtrelle was doing well in living with the symptoms from being diagnosed with lupus. From her research, she learned what can be triggers to cause a flare up. She took heed of those triggers and did her best not to do those things that would cause a flare up. Camtrelle had been getting her physical, mental, and spiritual life in order, but she started to feel a little lonely. She had been by herself for two to three years where she had no one and did not mess around with anyone. Camtrelle wanted a companion. She had done many things by herself like going out to eat, going to the movies, going to plays, and anywhere else she wanted to go. She no longer wanted to do those things by herself. Since Camtrelle did not put herself out there to meet anyone, she took to the familiar. She set her sights on someone at work. She wanted someone that would wine and dine her, treat her like a queen. Camtrelle thought that Elliott might be that guy, so she pursued him. Camtrelle flirted with Elliott until they exchanged numbers. They talked on the phone and got to know one another.

Camtrelle and Elliott took their time getting to know one another, and it turned into a relationship. Camtrelle had not been in a relationship since Josiah and her heart still had not healed. Camtrelle already knew in the back of her mind that she could not fully give herself to Elliott. The relationship between Camtrelle and Elliott progressed slowly. They had day dates all the time. Camtrelle was enjoying the companionship of having someone to do things with her. She started spending more time with Elliott. As Elliott came around more, Camtrelle thought about her child. No man other than Josiah had ever met her child. The only way Camtrelle would introduce someone to her child was if he were going to be around long term. It appeared that Elliott would be in Camtrelle's life long-term.

One thing that Camtrelle liked about Elliott was his relationship with his mother. He talked to her every day and always ended the call letting her know he loved her. Camtrelle always thought that if a man loved his mom and treated her as a queen, he would know how to love and treat Camtrelle as a queen. Something else that Elliott did that caught Camtrelle's attention was seeing Elliott read the Bible. Believing in God was important to Camtrelle if she was going to be in a relationship with someone. When Elliott took Camtrelle on a weekend trip to introduce her to some of his family, the first place they went was to worship service. Camtrelle would never forget how she had to stand up as a visitor and introduce herself and the place of worship where she was a member. The service was good, and afterwards, they went to Elliott's brother's house where Camtrelle met two of his siblings and their spouses. His family was very welcoming and Camtrelle felt comfortable being herself around them. There were other family gatherings where Camtrelle was introduced to more of Elliott's family members and eventually met his children.

Elliott was great with Camtrelle's child. They established a relationship and Camtrelle knew she could trust Elliott when it came to her child. They would spend time together doing different things without Camtrelle. They had built a bond which made Camtrelle happy. Elliott was a wonderful father to his kids, and he treated Camtrelle's child as one of his own. He was able to fill a void in her child's life when the biological did not hold true to his commitments. Camtrelle was glad she had Elliott in her life. She could see a future with him, although she knew she would be settling. Elliott was a good man to Camtrelle and her child, but he was not the man for her. Camtrelle's mom also gave the thumbs up to Elliott. She liked him and gave her full approval. He was the type of man she wanted in Camtrelle's life. He was mature and stable. He could provide for Camtrelle and her child. He could protect them and be more of an influence in their lives.

Elliott was good to Camtrelle. During the worst times of Camtrelle dealing with health issues from the lupus diagnosis, Elliott was there. He would do anything that Camtrelle may have needed from picking up prescriptions to taking her to doctor's appointments. When Camtrelle had to have surgery, he was right by her side to do whatever was needed. Camtrelle was grateful for all he had done for her and her child. Camtrelle had been in a relationship with Elliott for more than two years, but it would not last.

Once again, Camtrelle had someone in her life that experienced a terrible loss. Elliott had a death in the family that would be life changing to his and Camtrelle's relationship. Camtrelle did not know what to say or do to help Elliott during this time. She did not know how to comfort him. She had experienced loss in her life before, but Camtrelle looked at death differently than most people, so her reaction to it was different. Camtrelle knew she should have been doing something, but she was clueless as to what to do. Camtrelle had also messed up with Elliott by introducing him to Josiah. What was Camtrelle thinking to do such a thing? It was a big mistake. The relationship went downhill. The entire tone of the relationship changed. Camtrelle could tell that trust issues entered the relationship after Elliott met Josiah, although nothing was said outright. They began to argue all the time about anything and everything. He would be mad, and she would be mad. They would even bring the attitudes with them to work. They both knew that the relationship had become unhealthy, so it eventually ended and faded into a lasting friendship.

Camtrelle had adapted to the darkness of her work environment like many others by having a relationship with a coworker. Because so much time is spent at the job, friendships are established and sometimes they lead into relationships. Camtrelle had seen couples in long-term relationships where they are both married to other people. There were also couples where only one of them is married. Sometimes those relationships would get complicated. There were always short-term affairs. The darkness at the workplace was a breeding ground for all types of sinful relationships. Camtrelle witnessed how spouses that work together would cheat on one another or just one of them cheat right under their spouse's nose. She saw spouses get divorced only to marry someone else within the company, in many cases, where the people involved knew one another. The relationships would occur across all levels. No one was exempt. One would hope that the endings to those relationships were amicable because you continue to have to see and work with one another. Everyone would be attacked at some point, whether it was something said that was inappropriate, to a little flirting, to the way a person touched you or got in your space. Camtrelle had entered the darkness, was overcome by it, and then adapted to it. Her senses had adjusted to the darkness to where she was able to see in the darkness, walk around in it, and operate in it.

The Reversion

Camtrelle was now prickly aware of the surrounding darkness. When she entered those turnstiles, she could feel the thickness of the atmosphere. Even before entering the building, just being in the parking lot changed her demeanor. People would often ask her why she was frowning when she did not even realize that she was frowning. As a result, many people thought Camtrelle was mean. Camtrelle just did not like mess or want to be involved and caught up in mess. She had enough of her own mess to deal with, so she did not want to deal with others. After her relationship with Elliott ended, Camtrelle chilled out for a while. She just wanted to live her life in peace. When she was at work, she stayed to herself. She did her job, then went home. When she was home, she spent time with her mother and child. Camtrelle always wanted more for herself so she decided she would go back to school. She wanted to get her master's degree. Getting her master's was not about anyone but Camtrelle. It was something she wanted to accomplish for herself.

Camtrelle had been living her life going through the motions. Deep down, she was depressed. She had gone down some wrong paths and did not like or love herself from the decisions she had made. She would go home and just lie across her bed not wanting to get up or do anything. She did not want to live any longer, but she knew that there were people who needed her to still be here. Camtrelle believed in God, had faith in God, knew the power of God, but God was not her issue. She no longer believed in herself or had faith in herself. Camtrelle's issues were internal. Camtrelle knew that the only way she would come out of the depression was with the help of God.

Writing was therapeutic for Camtrelle, so she would write just to get her feelings out. Sometimes, she would cry and that would help her feel better. Some things she would share with her friends that she knew would not judge or condemn her. It felt good to Camtrelle to be able to talk about her feelings to people that would just listen to her, or comfort her, or offer advice when she asked. What helped her the most was listening to her gospel music. Camtrelle loved gospel music because it ministered to her soul and spirit. The songs would speak to her spirit and encourage her. The songs strengthened her and gave her hope. The music put her in remembrance of the God she served. There were no signs of what Camtrelle was going through. No weight gain or weight loss. No change in her attitude or the way she talked. There was nothing anyone could have picked up on that said she was depressed. Camtrelle was good at masking her feelings. Camtrelle slowly dug herself out of that hole because Jesus kept her. Camtrelle began to function again as a whole person.

Was Camtrelle a whole person? Not even close. Camtrelle was doing life but still had not put in the work to overcome the issues that plagued her. She did not take authority over her flesh. She did not apply the blood to cover her guilt or shame. She did not repent of her sins. She did not petition God to set her free where she would be free indeed. She did not ask God to cleanse her heart and renew a right spirit within her. She did not present her body as a living sacrifice. As a result, she conformed to the darkness within the walls of DDV Abyss Inc. Camtrelle was doing some on-the-job training when it happened yet again. Camtrelle saw Roland and knew she wanted to be with him.

This time was different for Camtrelle because she wanted him physically. That had not been the case before. Next thing you know, Camtrelle had reverted to her old ways and her old pattern. She started flirting with Roland to get his attention. Roland took the bait. Camtrelle would talk to Roland at work to get to know him, but there were not any other conversations outside of work. This was cool with Camtrelle because Roland had a girlfriend and Camtrelle did not want to be part of any drama. After some time had passed, Camtrelle and Roland decided it was time to get together. This is when they exchanged numbers. Camtrelle went over to his place and things went down. Camtrelle was not disappointed.

Camtrelle was not trying to continue to be with him. She was with him and that was all she wanted. Camtrelle knew this was a road she did not want to go down again but did not feel strong enough to stop herself. She needed God to step in. God stepped in and gave Camtrelle a wakeup call, which is what Camtrelle needed. Camtrelle vowed to make a change in her life. Camtrelle kept her vow until.

Camtrelle was doing well when the tempter showed himself. Camtrelle was aware of his usual tactics. Resist the devil and he will flee. When the tempter comes, God has already made a way of escape. When tempted, speak the word of God, "It is written..." Camtrelle knew this, yet she did none of it. Camtrelle had gotten her life on course. She was not thinking about a man, thinking about a relationship, or thinking about sex. She had learned to be content in the state that she was in. She had gone years without a man in her life. She had male friends, but that was the extent of men in her life. She was proud of how far she had come. Out of nowhere it seemed, Logan started talking to her every time he saw her. Camtrelle did not think anything of it because it was never anything inappropriate or out of line. Camtrelle did not even find anything he said was flirtatious. He did not even look at her in any type of way. Camtrelle was cool with it.

Then there was a subtle shift. Logan started talking about God and his beliefs. Now talking about God was attractive to Camtrelle. Camtrelle still did not think anything of it because she had always been the one initiating things, so she did not recognize when someone was trying to get at her without being overt about it. Then the pattern started again. They exchanged numbers and would talk on the phone. Camtrelle never asked him if he was married, and he never spoke of a wife. They talked on the phone all the time, and Camtrelle could call him on the phone at any time. Camtrelle did make one change. Logan was never invited to Camtrelle's place. They would only talk on the phone or talk at work. They started spending more time together at work talking about the word. There it was, another subtle shift, spending more time together. The conversations slowly changed over time, and they became more personal.

Logan made his interest known and Camtrelle should have taken off in the other direction. She thought she was strong enough to overcome this test, but she was not. She failed miserably and was angry and disappointed with herself. She thought she had conquered the darkness, but her light went out once again. Camtrelle found herself on the way to meet Logan at a motel. She had time to turn around and cancel. Even when she got to the room, she could stop things from happening. It was one of the worst experiences ever, if not the worst. Camtrelle was watching Family Feud the entire time. She was anxious for it to be over with, which it did not last long anyway. Once it was over, Logan had this look on his face like he really enjoyed himself while Camtrelle was disgusted and wanted to hurry and get out of there. Camtrelle was so mad at herself for throwing away years of living holy for nothing. Things were never the same between Logan and Camtrelle after that encounter.

She could not look at him the same way. Camtrelle would do her best to avoid him. The phone calls became less and less until they no longer talked on the phone. Camtrelle later found out that Logan was indeed married. Their schedules were different, so that was how he was able to talk on the phone so much. Camtrelle had reached the end of her rope. She was determined to no longer let the darkness consume her. She was done with men at her workplace. There was to never be another after Logan. Camtrelle did not need the judgement of others. She judged herself harshly. Camtrelle had to take the same mindset of being in the world and not of the world when it came to her workplace. Although she worked in the darkness, she did not have to become the darkness or adapt to the darkness. Camtrelle wanted her light to shine before men, and she was going to do the work to make it happen. She had fallen, but she would get back up.

The Transformation

When Camtrelle got back up, she was ready to do the work. She was ready for change in every area of her life. Camtrelle knew she needed God to run her life because she was making a complete mess of it. Camtrelle wanted her steps to be ordered by the Lord and that was through following him in obedience. Camtrelle went to the Lord and repented of the things she had done. She had asked for forgiveness earlier, but now she was repenting. Repenting meant that Camtrelle was to do it no more. Camtrelle was determined to get things right in her life. The first area Camtrelle saw a change was financially. God increased her finances, which caused a manifested blessing in Camtrelle's life in being able to move from her apartment into a house. She no longer had to see Josiah or his wife, although she and Josiah were friends. That pain still ran deep. This home was going to represent a fresh start where Camtrelle could make new memories.

Camtrelle was moving physically, but she was still taking herself to her new place. She needed to become new and put on the new man. To put on the new man, Camtrelle had to transform her mind and transform her words. She had to apply the blood to cover the guilt, to cover the shame, to blot out her transgressions. She asked God to cleanse her from all unrighteousness. She had to put on the whole armor of God so she could stand against the wiles of the devils. Camtrelle did not want to go back down the same roads that she had been traveling. It was time for some new scenery, a new direction, a new destination, and a new ending to her story. Camtrelle was posturing herself to live after the Spirit instead of the lusts of the flesh. She knew that God had so much more for her, and she wanted everything that God had for her.

Camtrelle's eyes were wide open. The scales had fallen off. When she entered DDV Abyss Inc., she saw the enemy at work. He was using many people in many ways. There was no dignity and respect. There was no integrity. There was no honesty. Lies flowed off lips like currents flow in rivers. Talk about the backstabbing. Talk about the gossip and all the rumors. Talk about the harassment. Talk about the zero tolerance. There were so many different spirits roaming around that place. It was the enemy's playground. They sought the weak then devoured them. Camtrelle was being devoured by the darkness BUT GOD!!!

Camtrelle could no longer adapt to the darkness. She wanted the light to shine forth. She came to understand how God had protected her through all her sinful liaisons. She understood why God allowed some things to happen for some and not others. With Camtrelle having a greater understanding of what was occurring within her workplace environment, she was able to strengthen her resolve to be better and to do better. God brought people into her life that also wanted to shine their lights. Light always pushes out the darkness. As more of the darkness was pushed out of Camtrelle's life, there were still areas in her life where she had to apply the word and light up the darkness.

PART III: Lighting Up the Darkness

Camtrelle's healing had fully manifested, and she was no longer taking medication for lupus. She had stopped setting up follow-up appointments. Other health issues attacked Camtrelle's body. She went to see cardiologists, gastroenterologists, and gynecologists. Camtrelle did not understand at the time that many things that manifest in your physical body has to do with what is happening with you spiritually. Think about it: heart issues, digestive issues, and women issues. Camtrelle had not dealt with these areas spiritually. Camtrelle still had the resentment in her heart for Josiah. She would eat things that would bloat her, cause her weight gain, cause her abdominal pain because she was listening and hearing the word, but not releasing the word to others. She was not grabbing someone by the hand and pulling them out of the darkness along with her. She was not being a friend when she allowed her friends to continue on their destructive paths.

Camtrelle held onto what she was learning instead of sharing the goodness, grace, and mercy of our God. With the women's issues that Camtrelle suffered, such as the debilitating cramps, the heavy flow, and the biopsies, they represented for Camtrelle the unforgiveness of herself and others, her faith, and her trust in God and his process. The only way Camtrelle's physical life was going to improve was to improve her spiritual life. Camtrelle had to be willing to take her spiritual life to the next level.

Through it all, Camtrelle showed up for work. She did not like missing work, and she took very little time off. She was on a mission to build up her sick and vacation time. She wanted to have the time available if ever she needed to be off due to unforeseen circumstances. Camtrelle's work shift allowed her to go to appointments, attend her child's school events, and attend other events without having to use her vacation time. She only used her sick time when it was absolutely necessary. She was engaged at work and wanted to make a difference. Camtrelle had always been a self-motivated person, so she learned as much as she could from her coworkers and training. For Camtrelle, it was not about moving up but just having knowledge. She wanted to know the whys. Camtrelle was dedicated to her job, but she did not have it in its proper perspective. She gave so much of herself to it. She brought it home with her. It was in her thoughts and in her dreams. It was a major part of her conversations. It consumed her because Camtrelle wanted to be successful in accomplishing her goals and the goals of her job. The problem is the system is not designed for someone to experience success long-term. The environment at DDV Abyss Inc. is one that focuses on the negative. Nine out of ten goals could have been accomplished, and all the focus would be on the one that failed. It is not a bad thing to focus on the failure, but it is the way that it is done.

The beration, the degradation, and the humiliation that is gone through because there was a failure does not lead to success. Camtrelle had to change the narrative and think about the job differently. As Camtrelle's relationship strengthened with God, the job became to her a financial source and not her life. She was not going to continue to let people mistreat her or talk to her in a demeaning manner. Camtrelle was going to trust God to put her in the company of people that she needed to know. This would allow her to continue on her career path without having to do things that would make her question her morals.

As Camtrelle's life was starting to align more with the will of God, Camtrelle thought about her personal life. She always saw herself as married and making someone a good wife. She had a collection of lessons on marriage. She knew the scriptures on marriage. She felt she was ready for her husband to show up. She did not want to live her life alone, and she did not want to go back down wrong paths. One day, Camtrelle was driving on the freeway and having a conversation with God. She was telling God how she was ready for her husband and to send the one that he had for her. Camtrelle had always went after someone without asking God, so this time she wanted to make sure it was going to be different. She knew that God knew better than she did. Camtrelle did not pray for a husband or ask for anything specific in a man. She only wanted the one that God had designed for her. She asked God who was the one for her. Camtrelle had a belief that God introduces you to your mate at a young age, so you can commit yourself to that person and not establish soul ties with others.

We like to discount puppy love or teenage love because we feel like the maturity is not there. When you study some of the ages of the people in the Bible, they were young. With that said, God gave Camtrelle her answer and a picture of Josiah flashed. Camtrelle thought, God has a sense of humor. There is no way he is saying Josiah is the one for her. After what happened between them, there was no way God wanted Camtrelle with Josiah.

The Capitulation

Camtrelle was not expecting God's answer. She was caught off guard. To be with Josiah meant Camtrelle would have to deal with the pain, the hurt, the resentment, and anything else that she was holding against Josiah. Camtrelle did not know if she could do it or if she even wanted to do it. She and Josiah were friends, and Camtrelle could talk to him, but to be with him in a relationship again was mentally challenging for her. Camtrelle had a choice to make. Was she going to surrender to God's will in this area of her life, or was she going to do things her own way which always led to more hurt and pain for her? He had reached out to her years before, but Camtrelle could not move out of her own way.

She was in her flesh when it came to him. Camtrelle had already been talking to Josiah on the phone, so the difficulty would be to talk about their past in the present, so they could move forward in their future. Camtrelle had been talking to Josiah about another guy, Evan. Camtrelle would have gone down that path again. The difference was Evan was long distance, and God used Josiah to bring Camtrelle to her senses. Camtrelle had always been able to talk to Josiah about anything and everything, and he never did judge her or condemn her. He was her best friend and Camtrelle did miss the friendship they had. Camtrelle started talking to Josiah more and Evan less. Camtrelle was still struggling because she should have stopped talking to Evan altogether since he was married, and she was trying to reestablish a connection with Josiah.

Camtrelle noticed that God put her and Josiah right back at the place where they messed up before. The circumstances were eerily similar to where they began the first time. Josiah was getting out of a relationship, and Camtrelle had to wait patiently for things to be finalized before Josiah could be with her. Camtrelle was not a patient person, and God had to do much work on her in that area. Josiah also had pent-up feelings regarding Camtrelle, so he was not in a rush since he was just getting out of a marriage. This second time around was not going to be easy. Because Josiah was to be the last man in Camtrelle's life, Camtrelle had things she had to go through with Josiah because of all the wrong things she had done in other relationships. Josiah had done some things that he needed to set right. Camtrelle lacked understanding at the time, so it caused more issues in the relationship. Camtrelle felt like she was not a priority in his life. Josiah had his work, his children, his mother, and whatever else he was dealing with in his past relationships. Camtrelle did not feel he had time for her. Josiah would come see her for a short time, which was never long enough for Camtrelle.

They would talk around their past and mistakes that were made, but nothing was ever resolved. The pain was still there, and more pronounced now that she had Josiah back in her life. He had his mixed feelings as well. Camtrelle felt a cycle of being hurt over and over again by this man that God said was her mate. Camtrelle was mad with God. She did not want to understand why this was happening in her life. She knew why it was happening, but she still did not want to have to go through it. So many times, she wanted to leave. Just say forget it and be by herself. There was times Josiah wanted to leave also. Camtrelle shed many tears. As long as she and Josiah were in the flesh and not addressing what was in their hearts, things were not going to get better between them, and they were going to stay right there in their mess until they got it right.

It was a long, enduring process. Years of tearing down the walls and fences that were built up. Years of destroying a foundation that was not built upon God. Camtrelle and Josiah knew that they could get through it, as long as they kept God first in their lives and kept God first in the relationship. Camtrelle was strengthened every time she wanted to leave. For the joy set before her, she endured. For the lesson she was learning about patience having her perfect work, she endured. For the lesson of being molded individually while being yoked together, she endured. For the lesson of nevertheless, Camtrelle endured. For the lessons of trusting and believing God, she endured. For the lesson of developing her faith, Camtrelle endured. For the lesson of love, she endured.

At the workplace, there was more disappointment. At some point, if there is a desire to move up or just do something different, getting screwed over at least once is going to occur. The stories were told time and time again from people who eventually were able to move up in their careers. It was not about skill or ability, but who you know and whether or not the people who got to make the decisions liked you. Some people do not like you and do not know why they do not like you. Camtrelle had been through that several times. It was a blessing that Camtrelle did not realize at the time. What the enemy meant for evil, God worked it out for Camtrelle. Camtrelle was upset at the time when she knew she was done wrong, but she did not let it deter her. Negative thoughts crossed her mind, but she did not act on them. No good would have come from it. Camtrelle just moved on from it. She had learned that whatever task or work she did was unto the Lord and not man.

As a result, other opportunities came Camtrelle's way. She was fully persuaded to follow the course that had been charted for her. When opportunities arose, Camtrelle prayed about it. When her answer was yes, she said yes, and when the answer was no, Camtrelle turned down the opportunity. Many people had moved up in their careers quickly because they were willing to do things of the dark. Camtrelle was willing to work the process and move at a pace that was sustainable and fulfilling. When the light is on the rise, darkness has to go. The capitulation was taking place in every area of Camtrelle's life.

The Illusion

Camtrelle's child was now in those years of adolescence where he was learning about life and finding out who he wanted to be. With Camtrelle's shift being at night, she had to trust that her child was going to make decisions that would not have a negative impact on his life or cause her to have an adverse reaction towards him. Camtrelle wanted him to have independence with boundaries, if that makes sense. Every time he walked out the door, Camtrelle covered him with the blood of Jesus. He would come home at times with a swollen hand or other marks that represented a fight. Camtrelle did not know what he was doing, but she continued to pray for him. They had always been able to talk, but Camtrelle knew he was not going to be truthful about what was going on in his life. Most of time, he was home playing video games or with friends playing basketball.

He was on his school's football team, but that was not his thing. Camtrelle just wanted to make sure that she supported him in whatever he wanted to do. Academics were not his thing either. Camtrelle wanted him to be more like her when it came to school, but he was more like his father. Camtrelle saw the potential in him and knew he was smart, if he would just apply himself. It was a stressful time for Camtrelle. Camtrelle would sow targeted seeds towards his education and career. She had learned how seeds can be targeted for a specific purpose. It worked, and she continued to sow seeds for other purposes. As he was maturing, he would struggle with keeping a job.

Camtrelle did not understand why at the time, but she later gained insight. Camtrelle and her son would go to services. There was a time when he did not want to go, but Camtrelle did not give him a choice.

Camtrelle was going to train him up in the way that he should go. Then there was a shift. He would be ready to go to service before Camtrelle. He would pay attention to the lesson and remember something that was said. He was beginning to have a desire to know the things of God. He and Josiah had a great relationship. Josiah had been there from the beginning. Josiah was there to help answer questions he was having about God. They would talk for hours about God and other subjects that Camtrelle was not privy to know about. Camtrelle would smile on the inside while watching the bond that they shared. Josiah always treated Camtrelle's child as if he were his own. One thing about Camtrelle's child is that he was spoiled. He had an extremely close relationship to his granny. She did anything and everything for him. Every time Camtrelle turned around, his granny was buying him something. Camtrelle would try to stop her but it never worked. She eventually just gave up and would take things from him when talking no longer worked. The relationship changed with his granny once she got married. Her husband was delusional, and it affected all of her relationships. Camtrelle felt like she was stuck in the middle. She did not know the undercurrents that were ebbing inside of her child.

Before Camtrelle's mother got married, it was always the threesome: Camtrelle, her son, and her mother. Camtrelle's mother was always there to help Camtrelle, no matter the reason. Camtrelle did not know what she would have done without her. She was such a blessing to Camtrelle. Camtrelle could not do enough for her mother to show her how much she loved and appreciated her. She had done so much to help Camtrelle. She and Camtrelle did everything together. She was her BFF. Like Camtrelle, her mother did not talk about things that were going on in the inside. As Camtrelle's child got older, he was gone from the house more and more. This would leave Camtrelle's mother at the house alone. Camtrelle did not know that she was afraid to be in the house alone. She would take medication to help her sleep, or she would stay up and walk around the house when she did not want to take the pills.

Camtrelle's mom started having seizures and Camtrelle did not know why. She had never suffered from seizures before. It scared Camtrelle. Come to find out, it was the sleeping pills that were causing the seizures. Camtrelle felt so guilty because she did not know her mom was afraid. She would have done something differently if she would have known. It weighed heavily on Camtrelle. When the love of her life was brought back into her life, Camtrelle's mom was the happiest, and she deserved all the happiness she could handle. Camtrelle could see how her mother had someone to lean on, someone to make her feel that everything was going to be fine, someone to take care of her wants and needs, and someone to make her feel that special kind of love.

She was no longer afraid because she now had him. After several years of enjoying married life, Camtrelle's mom's life changed. Her husband suffered a stroke, and he could no longer walk or care for himself. Camtrelle's mom did what she could to take care of him, but it became too much for her. Their son Waylenn would come by the house and help care for his dad. They eventually moved back to Camtrelle's grandparents' home where their other son Glayne was living. Glayne was a great caretaker. Glayne was able to see about the needs of both his parents. Camtrelle was saddened by not having her mother with her any longer, but she knew it was for the best. Camtrelle's mother wanted to be back home. Camtrelle was comforted by the fact that a family member was always with her mother. Her husband had another stroke where he was admitted to the hospital and later transitioned from this life.

Camtrelle's mother was not the same after his passing. The light had gone out of her eyes. She was a shell of who she once was. She was heartbroken. Camtrelle went to visit her mother but not often enough. She would talk to her every day. Camtrelle tried to get her mom to come back and live with her, but she wanted to remain home. She transitioned from this life in her sleep where she wanted to be. Camtrelle was strong for a long time after losing her mother, but she eventually broke. Camtrelle was depressed for months. Her mother was gone, her son had moved out, and she was still having issues with Josiah. Camtrelle stopped going to worship service and was not even watching services online. God allowed this to go on until he said ENOUGH!

Camtrelle and Josiah's relationship was growing stronger but still was not where it needed to be. They were both still in their own way. They were alike in so many ways. Camtrelle would respond to his actions or inactions in a negative way, then he, in return, would do the same. Instead of resolving an issue, it would only get worse. The communication from Camtrelle was lacking. She held so much on the inside that Josiah was not aware of. It just kept building over time because she did not want to deal with it. Camtrelle felt she would say things that she could not take back, and she never wanted that to happen so she would not say anything. Josiah would get upset because Camtrelle would not express herself. He would communicate more, but there were things he still was not saying. He was holding on to things inside as well. Until they both were ready to talk about their truths, they would continue in a vicious cycle.

Camtrelle and Josiah had discussed marriage and Camtrelle thought she was ready, but deep inside she knew she was not. She did not want to go into a marriage feeling the way she did. She loved Josiah but did not trust him in the sense that she felt he was keeping things from her. Camtrelle did not know what it was, but she felt it. She still had the negative feelings of the past circling around in her head and heart that she did not openly talk about with Josiah. Every now and then, she would say how she was feeling, and the conversation would go left. There were numerous times where Camtrelle wanted to give up on the relationship, but she always remembered what God said. Camtrelle was certain there were times Josiah wanted to end the relationship, but he held on to hope. He kept the faith and believed in the promises of God.

When Camtrelle saw that marriage could possibly be near, she was fearful. Camtrelle had been doing things her way all her life. She could come and go as she pleased and did not have to answer to anyone. She could buy what she wanted to buy when she wanted to buy it. She did not have to share her space. If she did not want to do something, she did not have to do it. She would have to leave her worship center and follow Josiah. Josiah was answering the call of God in his life, and he wanted to be sure Camtrelle was on board. The fear, another ploy of the enemy, of a lifestyle change sent Camtrelle down a familiar path.

Lionel made an inappropriate comment to Camtrelle. She was shocked by the comment and thought she got him straight. He did not make another inappropriate comment, but every day he would say something to her. Of course, Lionel worked with Camtrelle, so here we go again. Camtrelle would say something smart or sarcastic back to him, and it went from there. Camtrelle was feeling Josiah did not have time for her with his job, his children, and anything else he was doing. His time was taken up and Camtrelle only received a small portion of it. Camtrelle could not understand how she was to be his wife if she felt she did not even fit into his life. The attention and time Lionel was giving her, Camtrelle felt was lacking from Josiah. Camtrelle fell into the trap again. She spent her days talking to him on the phone and getting to know him. Camtrelle found similarities between Lionel and Josiah, which is what the enemy wanted her to see.

It confused Camtrelle. She started to rationalize that maybe God only wanted her with Josiah to cleanse her heart, so she would be fully able to give herself to someone else. She was not saying this for the sake of being with Lionel, but just knowing that she was going through a process that was almost over. Camtrelle did like Lionel in the way that he was a cool person. He was someone that Camtrelle could have fun with. He had a sense of humor. Camtrelle never saw anything long-term with him. Lionel had someone in his life that he had been with for years. She wanted to be married, but he did not want to get married, according to Lionel. Camtrelle realized what a mistake she was making with Lionel and prayed that it did not destroy her relationship with Josiah. Camtrelle told Josiah about Lionel and what she had been doing. She asked him to forgive her. Josiah was hurt, angry, in disbelief, and so much more.

Camtrelle felt terrible for hurting Josiah. Her acts of selfishness brought them back to the beginning. This time the outcome would be different. Josiah would forgive her. It was only the greater God in him that did not allow him to submit to the flesh. Camtrelle had much work to do to repair the relationship. Camtrelle had everything she wanted in Josiah, but the enemy will always put an illusion in her life where something or someone appeared better or greater than what she had. Seeing the illusion for what it is allows for illumination.

The Illumination

Camtrelle had to look in the mirror and ask herself some tough questions. She did not like the answers. Camtrelle had a relationship with God, but it was not intimate enough. She relied on everyone but Him to take care of her wants and needs. Her mother was such a rock for her and now she was gone. Her son was living his life and on his own. Josiah was doing the work in himself, so he was not available like Camtrelle thought she needed him to be. She had to learn to rely on God in a way that she did not have to before. She had to trust God. Camtrelle's life was not going to be rewarded until she diligently sought him. She started spending more time with God and developing their relationship. God was giving her revelations and understanding about questions that she had long awaited answers. She began to see the amazement of God's word. She started increasing her prayer life, and as a result, she built up a boldness within her. Camtrelle declared the word for herself and others. She prayed for others more than herself. Camtrelle was beginning to operate in her ministry.

****

Camtrelle's child was accepting the call on his life. He had established the relationship he always wanted with his father. Jeremy was operating in his ministry along with his wife, and they were mentoring Camtrelle's child. During this time, Camtrelle's child felt the need to separate himself from Camtrelle and Josiah. Camtrelle did not understand it, but she was strong through it. She had a peace that surpassed all understanding. It was through the power of God that she made it through that storm. God had prepared her for that time. Every Sunday at service, God would give her a word that would carry her through the week. God knows what you have need of before you know. Camtrelle was not angry, although she was hurt. She knew that all things were working together for good. She gave her child the time and space he needed for himself. Camtrelle was so Godly proud of him. He and his wife worked alongside their parents in ministry. They had their primary jobs along with businesses they had started. Camtrelle's child had an entrepreneurial mind and gifted talents that allowed him to showcase his creativity. His wife had a brilliant mind of her own and was supportive of the vision of her husband. She was a blessing to his family. Camtrelle believed that they had a powerful ministry within them that would have a great impact on his generation. As they continued to grow in the knowledge of God and his kingdom, favor and blessings abounded in their lives. Looking at her son's life, Camtrelle recognized that it should have been her and Josiah. God still had a plan for them. It took much work and effort, but Camtrelle and Josiah were in position to be a blessing to others and make an impact. Once they made a decision for God to work on them individually instead of telling God to fix the other person, things began to come together.

They both had God first in their lives, so they were able to build a foundation based on the word of God. The previous foundation had to be completely destroyed. There was no repairing but a rebuilding. They had reached a place where they could reveal what was in their hearts without it negatively affecting the relationship or hurting the other person. They were able to purge themselves of the pain and unforgiveness. Then a shift took place. Camtrelle saw God in Josiah like never before. She saw him walking in his calling and being elevated. Josiah was always in the word, studying the word, teaching the word to others, talking about God in all of his conversations, but it was at a greater level. Camtrelle's heart overflowed with love when she saw this. When a man is following God, a woman has no problem following him. Camtrelle would follow Josiah as he followed God. Camtrelle and Josiah went through a process that would allow them to be a testament to others and help them to overcome obstacles in their own relationships. Camtrelle and Josiah worked together in the ministry to bring God's will to pass though the vision given to Josiah. Josiah had already established his ministry of obedience, dominion, and power. Camtrelle was excited about their future because the latter is always greater than the former.

Camtrelle's light was going to shine everywhere, including her workplace. Camtrelle's light was the knowledge she had about the kingdom of God. The revelations she had been given to share with others. The darkness was the ignorance that was prevalent within that environment. People perish for a lack of knowledge. Camtrelle was going to share her insight in every way possible. She wanted to be used by God. Camtrelle's language changed, her attitude changed, her perspective changed, her thoughts changed; Camtrelle had been transformed, forgiven, redeemed, justified, delivered, and purged all by the grace of God. She kept her armor on so she could stand against the enemy's tactics. The void that she had been feeling was filled with the love of God.

It is in him that Camtrelle lived, moved and had her being. She was able to see God in the little things. Camtrelle did not say all of that to say that she was better than anyone else. She still had struggles, she still had trials and tribulations, she still sinned and fell short. We all will as long as we are in this flesh. Camtrelle desired for her spirit to have more victories than her flesh. Many of her defeats took place at the workplace, so what better place to become victorious and have the victories outweigh the defeats. It was past time for Camtrelle to show the enemy that he had already been defeated. Camtrelle was going to shine that light right in his eyes and shake the keys in his face.

Epilogue

DDV Abyss Inc is a good place to work. It provides stability and longevity. It provides the lifestyles that people desire, but it comes at a cost. There is sacrifice of time, family, friends, hobbies, services, and self. Do not be detoured from working at this company because it is just an example of what happens in most workplaces. It has been good in many ways, but it can get better. It is time for the light to shine within the walls of the facilities. The light will shine when the people start letting their light shine. We are the salt of the earth and light of the world. We are to be change agents for the changes that need to take place.

The change has to take place in the setting, in the tone, in the focus, in the process, in the communication. We must stand up for righteousness. We must stand up for who we are in Christ. The devourer has to be rebuked. We must remember that we are overcomers. When we fight, we win. We win against the system, not the people. The system is the darkness, and we know who rules the darkness. For we wrestle principalities, rulers of the darkness, and spiritual wickedness. We must close the portals that allow the darkness to enter. The light shone forth when it was said, let there be light. Decree and declare that there will be light shining forth in our lives that will affect change in all of our environments. Hold up the light and to God be the glory!

Conclusion

The purpose for writing this book is to help anyone that is struggling in life know that they are not alone, and it is possible to overcome. Everyone has made mistakes and bad decisions, but those choices, those decisions do not define us. As long as there is breath in your body, the opportunity is present to get on the right path and chart a course for your life that is guided by God. With God, all things are possible. If you have focused on the different people Camtrelle has been involved with, you have missed the mark. This story has been about someone who has struggled with many issues that others have faced in life and how her environment played a big part in how she dealt with those issues. It is about someone that says she is a Christian and has made Jesus Lord of her life but kept doing her will instead of submitting to his will. It is about someone that was stubborn and selfish and in denial about it. It is about someone that is allowed to be weak and vulnerable instead of showing strength and being guarded all the time. It is about someone that kept allowing her emotions to dictate her behavior then regretting the decisions she made from her emotions. It is about someone that was struggling with being carnal versus being spiritual. It is about God allowing you to continue to make the same mistakes until you learn the lessons, until you prove him. It is about someone overcoming her issues and finding the love, peace, joy, and strength of the Lord.

Personal Writings

In my struggles, God has allowed me to express myself in my writings. I have added these writings in hopes that it will help and bless others. They are more in depth in the word of God in order to overcome those struggles. We serve an Awesome, Amazing, Almighty God. When we are facing situations in life, we have to remind ourselves of who God is and who we are in Him. We have to believe that we will get through the storm if God allowed the storm to come into our lives. We should be a testimony of coming out of the storm better than we went in and giving God all the glory.

My Testimony: What Do You Do?
The Woman with the Issue of Blood

(Foundational Text: Mark 5:25-34)

Like the woman with the issue of blood, we have all faced sickness, illness, or some type of disease. The doctors' offices are filled with patients who have made appointments because they are dealing with some type of ailment. The hospitals are filled with patients that are suffering because of an accident, genetics (a history of a family disease that has been passed on through generations), the choices they made in life, and just because of life circumstances. There are hospices filled with patients who are dying of cancer. Mental institutions are filled with people who are suffering from some neurological defect. Now we ask ourselves, why are so many suffering? If there is a God, why is he allowing this to happen since he is omni-present, omnipotent, and omniscient?

The answer to your question is that God has given man free will and it's up to us to make Him Lord of our lives and exercise our faith and trust in him. Many people are suffering because they don't even believe in God, while others allow Satan to have victory over them; and yet still, we have believers who have put their faith and trust in someone other than God. Psalms 34:19 says that, *"Many are the afflictions of the righteous; but the Lord delivereth him out of them all."* You have to believe that he will deliver you out of every situation that you face in life. The woman with the issue of blood went to many different physicians and used all her resources, and still wasn't healed of the issue. It was only when she looked to Jesus that she was healed and delivered from her infirmity.

When we feel sick or have certain symptoms, what do we do? Ask our spouse, parents, friends, co-workers, siblings what they think may be wrong. The first thing we've done wrong is to go to them. We have allowed them to speak all kinds of things over us. Your symptoms sound like you may have this or that, or possibly that, or even worse, it could be this. We even get on the internet now and attempt to do a self-diagnosis. Then all of sudden, we're nervous and anxious because we've allowed them to put all these things in our head or we read something that has the symptoms we're experiencing. Philippians 4:6 says, *"Be careful for nothing; but in everything by prayer and supplication with thanksgiving let your requests be made known unto God."*

This means don't have anxiety, don't fret, don't worry about your situation, but go to God in prayer with thanksgiving in our hearts. We then should start speaking to those symptoms, to our mind, and body and confess the word. Isaiah 53:5 says, *"But he was wounded for our transgressions, he was bruised for our iniquities: the chastisement of our peace was upon him; and with his stripes we are healed."* We are the healed. He bore all of our sicknesses and diseases upon the cross, and sickness and disease have no authority or power over us. He is Jehovah Rapha. He is the God that healed thee. We must believe that we are healed and start praising Him in advance for our healing. Mark 11:22-24 says, *"And Jesus answering saith unto them, Have faith in God. For verily I say unto you, That whosoever shall say unto this mountain, Be thou removed, and be thou cast into the sea; and shall not doubt in his heart, but shall believe that those things which he saith shall come to pass; he shall have whatsoever he saith. Therefore, I say unto you, What things soever ye desire, when ye pray, believe that ye receive them, and ye shall have them."* You will have what you say.

So, if you're saying I feel sick, guess what, you're going to feel sick. If you keep claiming that you have some disease, then guess what, you're going to have that disease. We still must do everything in the natural while God does the supernatural. Go to your doctor, fill your prescription, take your medicine, but at the same time, you have to speak the Word over your situation. I am the healed. My body and mind function as it was designed to function. Thank you, God, for healing me. You are Jehovah Rapha. While you are confessing the word and believing everything you're saying, God is working on the inside and doing the supernatural. In 1998, I was diagnosed with lupus. I didn't know what was going on with me. I couldn't do my job. I called in all the time. I was in pain all of the time and feeling tired all the time.

Then one day my co-worker said, you may have lupus. I went and did some research and said, I think this is the answer. I made an appointment with a rheumatologist and had some tests run. The test came back positive for lupus. I didn't get discouraged, scared, or depressed. I was actually glad that I knew what I was dealing with. I listened to the doctor tell me what all I needed to do, and I took the medicine that was prescribed for me. I did what he said, but at the same time I was talking to God as well. I had read stories about other people dealing with lupus and how debilitating it can be and how sick you can become to the point of death. I remember telling my mom and she started crying. I told her not to cry because I was going to be fine. How many of you know that the devil is a liar? I prayed, confessed the word, and praised God for my healing. It didn't manifest right away. I had one really bad year and some occasional flares for the next few years. I kept the faith. Lupus wasn't going to keep me from living. There is a name above all names. Philippians 2:10 says *"Wherefore God also hath highly exalted him, and given him a name which is above every name: That at the name of Jesus every knee should bow, of things in heaven, and things in earth, and things under the earth; And that every tongue should confess that Jesus Christ is Lord, to the glory of God the Father."* Jesus' name is above all names, so when you call on His name, all other names have to bow. Lupus had to bow.

Whatever you're going through or facing, it has to bow when the name of Jesus is called. Cancer has to bow, diabetes has to bow, AIDS has to bow, migraines have to bow, vertigo has to bow. It may not be a sickness. Bankruptcy has to bow, foreclosure has to bow, divorce has to bow, infidelity has to bow, homosexuality has to bow; whatever the name, it has to bow at the name of Jesus. Demons tremble at the name. Satan flees at the name. Call on Him. Lupus bowed at the name, and I can say that I haven't had a symptom, flare, or anything else that looks like lupus in at least eight years. It may be even longer. I'm here to say don't give up, don't give in. The manifestation is on the way. Just keep believing. I'm a living witness that God is real, and he is the God that heals.

Now in my situation, I listened to my co-worker, but my co-worker was also a fellow worship center member. If you're going to go to anyone about a situation you're facing in life, make sure that it is another believer and someone that has your best interests. You don't need anyone that is going to be negative and discourage you. You need people who are going to encourage and uplift you, who are going to pray for you earnestly, and who are going to be there for you in your hour of need.

What do you do when you go to the doctor, several doctors, and none of them have your answer like the woman with the issue of blood? Do you automatically think defeat or death sentence? Do you become depressed and suicidal? Do you blame God for what you're going through? Do you think that He is the one giving you the sickness or disease? Well, there is one doctor who has all the answers, and his name is Jesus. We tend to put too much faith in man when we should have our faith in Jesus. In 1993, I was away at school, and I had a sinus infection. I took some medicine and had an allergic reaction, and at the same time, found out I was pregnant. I was afraid to tell my mom because I knew she would be disappointed in me.

I also knew that fornication was a sin and that what I was doing was wrong, but my God is so gracious, merciful, and forgiving. I had to move back home from school. My brother and sister-in-law came and packed up all my things because I had so much pain in my hands from the allergic reaction. I could barely use them. The allergic reaction progressively got worse where I was walking with a cane or sometimes in a wheelchair because of all the pain in my feet. My entire body was swollen, and I didn't know if it was from the allergic reaction or the pregnancy. I went to all kinds of specialists trying to determine what was wrong with me. Being pregnant, I couldn't really take any medicines because they could have caused harm to my baby. I cried daily for three months because of all the pain.

I felt like God was punishing me for fornicating, but God doesn't make mistakes. Thank God for believers and laborers. I had people visiting me all the time praying for me, ministering to me, laying hands on me, and letting me know that God still loved me and he wasn't punishing me. John 10:10 says, *"The thief cometh not, but for to steal, and to kill, and to destroy: I am come that they might have life, and that they might have it more abundantly."* When we're going through a situation, we tend to focus on the situation and our circumstances instead of God. When we do this, our situation overwhelms us, and we forget who God is and what he is capable of doing. Jeremiah 32:17 says, *"Ah Lord GOD! behold, thou hast made the heaven and the earth by thy great power and stretched out arm, and there is nothing too hard for thee."* All throughout the Bible we see where Jesus went about healing the sick, casting devils out, raising the dead, and performing other miracles during his ministry on Earth. If he is doing the healing, why would he cause the sickness? Jesus doesn't put sickness on anyone.

With all the prayers I received, reading the word for myself, and watching Christian television, I was able to seek God and ask for forgiveness and forgive myself. Then one day, God spoke to me and said, put on some socks and tennis shoes--I hadn't been wearing anything but slippers or socks on my feet when I went to the doctor. I did it, and my feet instantly stopped hurting. I was pain-free and able to walk without assistance. No more problems after hearing from God. I never did find out from any doctors what was wrong, and my baby was born healthy with no problems. God is able. It was only when I turned to Jesus for myself did, I receive the manifestation of my healing. Jesus said he would never leave us nor forsake us; he is Jehovah Shammah, The Lord who is always there. He is just waiting on us to call upon Him.

What do you do when you feel and think that you're doing everything—you're praying, you're confessing, you're believing, you're praising—and there is still no manifestation. Remember, the woman with the issue of blood didn't receive her manifestation for twelve years. We must continually check ourselves. Are we harboring any unforgiveness in our hearts? Mark 11:25 says, *"And when ye stand praying, forgive, if ye have ought against any: that your Father also which is in heaven may forgive you your trespasses."* Not forgiving others will delay the manifestation of your healing. Are you married and you and your spouse are at odds with one another? 1 Peter 3:7 says, *"Likewise, ye husbands, dwell with them according to knowledge, giving honor unto the wife, as unto the weaker vessel, and as being heirs together of the grace of life; that your prayers be not hindered."* You and your spouse should be on one accord. You should be able to agree to disagree without it affecting your marriage to the point where your prayers are being hindered. Are you living a holy life? I Peter 1:15-16 says, *"But as he which hath called you is holy, so be ye holy in all manner of conversation; Because it is written, Be ye holy; for I am holy."* You have to repent and get the sin out of your life. We must be good stewards of this physical body in which we live. Romans 12:1-2 says, *"I beseech you therefore, brethren, by the mercies of God, that ye present your bodies a living sacrifice, holy, acceptable unto God, which is your reasonable service. And be not conformed to this world: but be ye transformed by the renewing of your mind, that ye may prove what is that good, and acceptable, and perfect, will of God."* We renew our minds by reading the word, studying the word, listening to the word, and living the word. James 1:22 says, *"But be ye doers of the word, and not hearers only, deceiving your own selves."* Let's begin to be doers, not just hearers.

One other testimony I would like to share about the healing power of God is that when I was a baby, I had epileptic seizures. The doctors told my mom I would be slow and have difficulties learning. I grew out of the seizures and excelled in school. I graduated high school with honors. I went on to complete school after having my baby and received my bachelor's degree. I was on the dean's list several semesters while pursuing this degree. I eventually went back to school and received my master's degree and graduated with a 3.9 GPA.

I'm not saying any of this to brag or boast of myself, but to give God the glory. All things are possible through him. He is able to do the exceedingly, abundantly above. When you're facing difficult situations in life, know that you have a partner who has your back. With God on your side, you're automatically a winner. You will be victorious in life and remember always to give Him the glory. By giving Him the glory, you will be glorified as well. Whatever you may be going through, know that you can turn that situation around with God's help. We go through things to make us stronger and to glorify God. Use your situation to bless someone else and become a testament to God's goodness.

Self Esteem: A Defining Moment / Self Reflection

Foundational Text:

Isaiah 10:27 *"And it shall come to pass in that day, that his burden shall be taken away from off thy shoulder, and his yoke from off thy neck, and the yoke shall be destroyed because of the anointing."*

Matthew 11:29-30 *"Take my yoke upon you, and learn of me; for I am meek and lowly in heart: and ye shall find rest unto your souls. For my yoke is easy, and my burden is light."*

A yoke can be defined as a frame fitting the neck and shoulders of a person, for carrying a pair of buckets or the like, one at each end. Instead of using buckets, imagine carrying on your right shoulder, low self-esteem, and on the left shoulder, a poor self-image. Many of us have suffered from low self-esteem. We felt unlikeable and unlovable. We did not feel worthy of having people show kindness towards us, did not feel worthy of having any true friends, did not feel worthy of even living at times. This low self-esteem was created in our minds due to our environment and circumstances. We allowed Satan to have a stronghold over our thoughts on how we see ourselves.

For many years, I allowed Satan to have control over my mind in this area and suffered from low self-esteem. I was a daddy's girl when I was really little. When the relationship ended with my dad and mother, that changed things between me and my dad. When you are young, you do not understand what happened and you think you did something wrong. This is what I did. I thought I did something wrong because my dad did not come around like he once did. I would talk to him, and he would always lie about seeing me and what he was going to do for me. I would often say to myself why doesn't he want to see me, why is he lying to me, and why won't he do anything for me. This is my father. He should want to have a relationship with me and help take care of me.

This is the beginning of the stronghold. Paul says in 2 Corinthians 10:3-5, *"For though we walk in flesh, we do not war after the flesh: (For the weapons of our warfare are not carnal, but mighty through God to the pulling down of strong holds;) Casting down imaginations, and every high thing that exalted itself against the knowledge of God, and bringing into captivity every thought to the obedience of Christ."* Ephesians 6:16 says, *"Above all, taking the shield of faith, wherewith ye shall be able to quench all the fiery darts of the wicked."* The fiery darts are the thoughts that Satan sends that goes against the will of God.

I was saved at a very early age and went to church all the time. I went to church with friends and went to bible study at a neighbor's house she had weekly for the kids of the neighborhood. Being so young, I didn't understand some of the things that were being preached and taught, but one of the first things you learn in Sunday school is: Jesus loves me this I know, for the Bible tells me so. I knew that I was loved. I felt loved, received love, but still wanted to feel and receive love from my father. He would tell me all the time that he loved me, but his actions didn't reflect love. I couldn't turn loose the thought that something was wrong with me because my dad didn't love me. Satan had this thought entrenched deep in my mind. As a result,

I had relationship problems. I went looking for love in all the wrong places and never found that fulfillment I was seeking.

Over the years, I kept in contact with my dad and was able to see him once I started driving. No matter what my dad said or did, I felt I still had to do my part to maintain a relationship. Ephesians 6:2-3 states, *"Honour thy father and mother; which is the first commandment with promise; That it may be well with thee, and thou mayest live long on the earth."* Growing up in the church, the Ten Commandments were another thing you were taught in Sunday school. The Ten Commandments can be found in Exodus, chapter 20. Exodus 20:12 says, *"Honor the father and thy mother: that thy days may be long upon the land with the Lord thy God giveth thee."* As you can see, honoring our parents can be found in the old and new testaments so it's a part of the old and new covenant with God. Knowing God's word, I knew that I had to respect and honor him. It was difficult and a constant battle. Matthew 26:41 says, *"Watch and pray, that ye enter not into temptation: the spirit indeed is willing, but the flesh is weak."*

My flesh wanted to tell him off, cuss him out, stay mad at him, hate him, but I couldn't do any of it. I knew I would have been wrong if I did any of those things, and it would have only made things worse for me; also, I wouldn't be here today because my dad wouldn't have tolerated any of it. Acts 8-21-23 says, *"Thou hast neither part nor lot in this matter: for thy heart is not right in the sight of God. Repent therefore of this why wickedness, and pray God, if perhaps the thought of thine heart may be forgiven thee. For I perceive that thou art in the fall of bitterness, and in the bond of iniquity."* This scripture refers to the sorcerer Simon attempting to purchase the power of the laying on of hands to receive the Holy Spirit, but I believe that it can apply to my situation. Although I was going through the motion of seeing and communicating with my dad, my heart wasn't right. I was still full of bitterness.

God allows things to happen in your life for a reason. I wasn't lacking in that I didn't receive what I would have needed from my father. God always will supply what you need. You just have to trust him. It may not come through your biological father, but He will place others around you to meet that need. A father is one who nurtures and develops a well-balanced person that will glorify God. A father's role is to protect, participate, prepare, provide, prophesy, pattern, and give perspective. Think back in your own lives and see if God provided a person or persons to fulfill this father's role in your life. In my life, I had my grandfather and my uncles. All my needs were met. I was protected. They didn't allow anything to happen to me. They participated. They taught me how to drive, took me places, and attended important events in my life. They prepared me for life by teaching me life lessons, making sure I was in church, and providing consequences (good/bad) for my actions. I was provided for. I had a roof over my head, clothes on my back, and never went hungry.

The men in my family knew the Word, even though sometimes you couldn't tell by their lifestyles. They would speak life into me. I was shown patterns of what to do and what not to do, how a man should be treated, how a man should treat a woman, and how a man should have God first in his life and lead his family. I was given perspective. I could go to them and get advice. I would listen to conversations and get perspective. I read the Bible to gain perspective. Everything I needed; God provided. Everything you need, God has already provided. You must learn how to access it and that's through the blood, through faith, and through his gift of grace.

You might ask how is it that she had low self-esteem if she knew the love of God and had all these people around her who loved her. I didn't confess the blood of Jesus over my thoughts in this area. I didn't ask him to cleanse me and make me whole in this area. I didn't repent of the negative thoughts I had against my father. As a result, I continued to make the same mistakes and feel the same way. 1 John 1:7, 9 says, *"... and the blood of Jesus Christ his Son cleanseth us from all sin...If we confess our sins, he is faithful and just to forgive us our sins, and to cleanse us from all unrighteousness."* Psalms 19:12 says, *"Who can understand his errors? Cleanse thou me from secret faults."* Psalms 51:1-3 says, *"Have mercy upon me, O God, according to thy lovingkindness: according unto the multitude of thy tender mercies blot out my transgressions. Wash me thoroughly from mine iniquity, and cleanse me from my sin. For I acknowledge my transgressions: and my sin is ever before me."* Acts 3:19 says, *"Repent ye therefore, and be converted, that your sins may be blotted out, when the times of refreshing shall come from the presence of the Lord."* To remove that yoke of low self-esteem, I needed to plead the blood of Jesus, ask for forgiveness, repent, and ask to be cleansed. I knew this, but guess what, I still didn't do it. I had held onto those thoughts for so long and felt that way for so long that I didn't know who and how I would be once I let those thoughts go. It was like an excuse I could use for the choices I made.

When my father died, I felt nothing at the time; with that, I really knew I had some deep-seated issues. I wasn't happy or sad. I tried to be there for my siblings as best I could. They were a little closer to him than I was. At the funeral, I met a couple of other brothers and sisters that I didn't know about. My sister read a poem at the funeral entitled Stranger. I said to myself, did anyone know this man? Many times, since his death I would find myself actually missing going by his home just to see him if it was only for a few minutes. Then one day, I was sitting in my bed, and I was watching a ministry on television and God spoke to me and said that he loved you the best he knew how. Instantly, all the ill feelings that I had toward my dad were gone. John 8:32 says, *"And ye shall know the truth, and the truth shall make you free."* I repented and asked for forgiveness. Thank God for his blood, his grace, and his mercy.

I was set free and delivered. John 8:36 states, *"If the Son therefore shall make you free, ye shall be free indeed."* I can honestly say I have love in my heart for my dad. We have to be the bigger person. Sometimes people just don't know how to love or how to show it because they never received it or were shown it. We must let them know what we need to feel loved by them; we then must receive it and in return, show it. 1 John 3:18 says, *"My little children, let us not love in word, neither in tongue; but in deed and in truth."* Your deeds are your actions. You can tell someone you love him, but if your actions don't reflect that love, then your words are meaningless. Loving in truth is loving through God because God is truth and God is love.

You can't tell someone that you love him if God is not a part of you. You don't truly know what love is. In John 14:6, *"Jesus saith unto him, I am the way, the truth, and the life: no man cometh unto the Father, but by me."* To speak truth, to speak life, you must have God in you and be a true believer that Jesus is the Son of God and that he died on the cross for our sins and rose again with all power in his hands, and that same power that he has, he gives to us for his glorification. 1 John 4:7-21 speaks on the source of love.

The Bible says, *"Beloved, let us love one another: for love is of God; and every one that loveth is born of God, and knoweth God. He that loveth not knoweth not God; for God is love. In this was manifested the love of God toward us, because that God sent his only begotten Son into the world, that we might live through him. Herein is love, not that we loved God, but that he loved us, and sent his Son to be the propitiation for our sins. Beloved, if God so loved us, we ought also to love one another. No man hath seen God at any time. If we love one another, God dwelleth in us, and his love is perfected in us. Hereby know we that we dwell in him, and he in us, because he hath given us of his Spirit. And we have seen and do testify that the Father sent the Son to be the Saviour of the world. Whosoever shall confess that Jesus is the Son of God, God dwelleth in him, and he in God. And we have known and believed the love that God hath to us. God is love; and he that dwelleth in love dwelleth in God, and God in him. Herein is our love made perfect, that we may have boldness in the day of judgment: because as he is, so are we in this world. There is no fear in love; but perfect love casteth out fear: because fear hath torment. He that feareth is not made perfect in love. We love him because he first loved us. If a man say, I love God, and hateth his brother, he is a liar: for he that loveth not his brother whom he hath seen, how can he love God whom he hath not seen? And this commandment have we from him, That he who loveth God love his brother also."* All of this is said so that we understand the true meaning of love.

With low self-esteem, you usually don't love yourself. How could I say I loved God when I really didn't feel worthy of love, and He created me in His image? Just by the mere facts that He created me, that His son died for me, and that I have life makes me worthy of love. Come what may, you must have a conviction in your heart that I am worthy of love just because of who I am and who my Father is, and I'm speaking on your heavenly Father. Don't let anyone tear you down and don't tear yourself down. Stand on His word, His truth. Once I truly believed and received who I was in Him, that yoke was destroyed.

That bucket of low self-esteem was taken off my neck and shoulders, and I am able to give love as well as receive it. That stronghold no longer exists and whatever dart Satan tries to throw my way hits the shield of faith and falls by the wayside. Tasha Cobbs has a song called "Break Every Chain". The song says there's power in the name of Jesus to break every chain. Everyone needs to know there is power in the name of Jesus to overcome every situation that you may face. Just start calling on the name of Jesus and receive your victory in faith. Start praising Him in advance for the victory is ours. The song goes on to say I hear the chains falling. You have to hear in the Spirit the chains and walls falling, the yokes being destroyed, the demons trembling, the trumpet sounding in your victory, Satan retreating, and the angels working on your behalf in whatever situation you may be facing. The manifestation is here. Just start believing and receiving. Rejoice in the Lord always, and again, I say rejoice.

Self-Examination: Building Your House
Foundational text: Matthew 7:24-27

Therefore, whosoever heareth these sayings of mine, and doeth them, I will liken him unto a wise man, which built his house upon a rock :25 And the rain descended, and the floods came, and the winds blew, and beat upon that house; and it fell not: for it was founded upon a rock. 26 And every one that heareth these sayings of mine, and doeth them not, shall be likened unto a foolish man, which built his house upon the sand: 27 And the rain descended, and the floods came, and the winds blew, and beat upon that house; and it fell: and great was the fall of it.

The weather has become unpredictable. It's sunny and hot one day, then cold and snowy the next. Places that don't normally get snow have seen snow. Tornadoes are rampant. Hurricanes forming before the season officially starts. Glaciers melting. Torrential rains and floods. City governments have building codes so your home can survive the elements. Insurance companies have policies to cover damage and losses caused by nature to your home. If you are planning to build a house on the rock, there are steps to building your house. The first step is to stake the lot. This means to survey the land and determine how you want to position your house to see if the land is a good place to even build a house. You may ask where is she going with this? What does this have to do with restoration?

Well, I'm going to show you step by step. When you first become interested in entering into the Kingdom of God and receiving salvation, you want to find a place where your soul and spirit can be fed. You stake the lot. You visit several places, some on your own while others are through the invitation of family and friends. You do this to determine if it's good ground to build your foundation. Are you going to grow spiritually and be able to stand against the enemy? Matthew 13:23 says, *"But he that received seed into the good ground is he that heareth the word, and understandeth it; which also beareth fruit, and bringeth forth, some a hundredfold, some sixty, some thirty."* We just learned that we want to be able to bear fruit. We must have a firm foundation that is built on good ground where the fruit of the spirit can grow. We received salvation according to Romans 10:9-10, *"9 That if thou shalt confess with thy mouth the Lord Jesus, and shalt believe in thine heart that God hath raised him from the dead, thou shalt be saved.10 For with the heart man believeth unto righteousness; and with the mouth confession is made unto salvation."* The second step in building your house is clearing and excavation. Some people have to be removed from your life.

Those frenemies, haters, hindrances. Some things have to be removed and some habits changed. What are you doing that's not pleasing in God's sight? Are you living a holy life? Are you living after the flesh instead of the spirit? Ephesians 4:20-24 says, *"But ye have not so learned Christ; 21 If so be that ye have heard him, and have been taught by him, as the truth is in Jesus: 22 That ye put off concerning the former conversation the old man, which is corrupt according to the deceitful lusts; 23 And be renewed in the spirit of your mind; 24 And that ye put on the new man, which after God is created in righteousness and true holiness."* The message translation makes it even clearer. *"20-24 But that's no life for you. You learned Christ! My assumption is that you have paid careful attention to him, been well instructed in the truth precisely as we have it in Jesus. Since, then, we do not have the excuse of ignorance, everything—and I do mean everything— connected with that old way of life has to go. It's rotten through and through. Get rid of it! And then take on an entirely new way of life—a God-fashioned life, a life renewed from the inside and working itself into your conduct as God accurately reproduces his character in you."* Sounds to me like some clearing and excavating.

Ridding yourself of the old man and becoming established in the new man. Our house is now ready to get some utilities, step three. With utilities we can get lights, we can get fire, there is a connection; in other words, we get power. Oh my God!!! We can have some power. Now to get this power, it requires permits. The good thing about receiving power is we are the ones giving the permits. The power for us is the Holy Spirit. We're growing in the knowledge and things of God. We've been cleansed, forgiven, reconciled to God, redeemed, justified all in two steps and now we have access to power.

John 20:21-22, *"²¹ Then said Jesus to them again, Peace be unto you: as my Father hath sent me, even so send I you.²² And when he had said this, he breathed on them, and saith unto them, Receive ye the Holy Ghost:"* Acts 1:8, *"But ye shall receive power, after that the Holy Ghost is come upon you: and ye shall be witnesses unto me both in Jerusalem, and in all Judaea, and in Samaria, and unto the uttermost part of the earth."* Acts 2:4, *"And they were all filled with the Holy Ghost, and began to speak with other tongues, as the Spirit gave them utterance."* Acts 2:38 says, *"Then Peter said unto them, Repent, and be baptized every one of you in the name of Jesus Christ for the remission of sins, and ye shall receive the gift of the Holy Ghost."* 1 John 2:27, *"But the anointing which ye have received of him abideth in you, and ye need not that any man teach you: but as the same anointing teacheth you of all things, and is truth, and is no lie, and even as it hath taught you, ye shall abide in him."* The anointing is the Holy Spirit. I gave several scriptures on the Holy Spirit because this is where many of us miss it. We don't ask for the gift of the Holy Spirit; we have the gift of the Holy Spirit and never open it, or we have opened the gift and don't use it. Your foundation has to have the Holy Spirit as a part of it, or it will sustain some costly damage, as we will see later in the text. The next step is the footings. This is the slab of concrete that is seen that supports the foundation of the house.

Our footing is the Word of God, the Bible. The Word of God has the answer for every situation we will face in life. Ecclesiastes 1:9 says, *"9 The thing that hath been, it is that which shall be; and that which is done is that which shall be done: and there is no new thing under the sun."* It has happened before, and it will happen again. The Word of God is our support. When you need encouraging, go to The Word. When you need uplifting, go to The Word. When you need a prayer answered, go to The Word. When you need Him to move suddenly in your life, go to The Word. Whatever you need, it's in The Word. When you need that support, listen to or read The Word. The word holds up the foundation. John 1:1, "In the beginning was the Word, and the Word was with God, and the Word was God." John 1:14 says, "And the Word was made flesh, and dwelt among us, (and we beheld his glory, the glory as of the only begotten of the Father,) full of grace and truth."

When you place the footing, which is the Word of God, the house will be able to stand. You have placed the weight of your house on God's truth. The Word of God is God. Now go back and replace The Word with God. The next step is the foundation.

What's important about the foundation is the material that it is made of, whether it be brick, concrete, or stone. What is your foundation going to be made of, the spirit or the flesh? Matthew 26:41 says, *"Watch and pray, that ye enter not into temptation: the spirit indeed is willing, but the flesh is weak."* Paul says in Romans 7:18-25, *"18 For I know that in me (that is, in my flesh,) dwelleth no good thing: for to will is present with me; but how to perform that which is good I find not. 19 For the good that I would I do not: but the evil which I would not, that I do. 20 Now if I do that I would not, it is no more I that do it, but sin that dwelleth in me. 21 I find then a law, that, when I would do good, evil is present with me. 22 For I delight in the law of God after the inward man: 23 But I see another law in my members, warring against the law of my mind, and bringing me into captivity to the law of sin which is in my members. 24 O wretched man that I am! who shall deliver me from the body of this death? 25 I thank God through Jesus Christ our Lord. So then with the mind I myself serve the law of God; but with the flesh the law of sin."* Romans 8:8-17 *"8 So then they that are in the flesh cannot please God. 9 But ye are not in the flesh, but in the Spirit, if so be that the Spirit of God dwell in you. Now if any man have not the Spirit of Christ, he is none of his. 10 And if Christ be in you, the body is dead because of sin; but the Spirit is life because of righteousness. 11 But if the Spirit of him that raised up Jesus from the dead dwell in you, he that raised up Christ from the dead shall also quicken your mortal bodies by his Spirit that dwelleth in you. 12 Therefore, brethren, we are debtors, not to the flesh, to live after the flesh. 13 For if ye live after the flesh, ye shall die: but if ye through the Spirit do mortify the deeds of the body, ye shall live. 14 For as many as are led by the Spirit of God, they are the sons of God. 15 For ye have not received the spirit of bondage again to fear; but ye have received the Spirit of adoption, whereby we cry, Abba, Father. 16 The Spirit itself beareth witness* with our spirit, that we are the children of God: *17 And if children, then heirs; heirs of God, and joint-heirs with Christ; if so be that we suffer with him, that we may be also glorified together."*

You can see why it's so important to have that footing established, to have The Word of God in your life. The flesh is powerful, but we can overcome the flesh with The Power of God and the Word of God. When we don't take a stand against our flesh, we can clearly see how we can get cracks in the foundation, which can become costly if the cracks are unnoticeable or just ignored. You will find that some cracks are just due to the settling of the foundation, learning through tests, trials, and tribulations. No cause for alarm at that time. The choice is ours as to the building blocks of our foundation, spirit or flesh. Next step is rough-in plumbing.

This is the installation of the water and sewer lines. These pipes are below the concrete. John 4:14, *"But whosoever drinketh of the water that I shall give him shall never thirst; but the water that I shall give him shall be in him a well of water springing up into everlasting life."* John 7:38 says, *"38 He that believeth on me, as the scripture hath said, out of his belly shall flow rivers of living water."* In order for the water to flow, the rough-in plumbing has to tap the source. The source is our Heavenly Father. Genesis 1:6-10, *"6 And God said, Let there be a firmament in the midst of the waters, and let it divide the waters from the waters. 7 And God made the firmament, and divided the waters which were under the firmament from the waters which were above the firmament: and it was so. 8 And God called the firmament Heaven. And the evening and the morning were the second day. 9 And God said, Let the waters under the heaven be gathered together unto one place, and let the dry land appear: and it was so. 10 And God called the dry land Earth; and the gathering together of the waters called he*

Seas: and God saw that it was good." As you can see, the spiritual and natural source was there from the beginning. When I look up the definition of source, one definition said the beginning or place of origin of a stream or river. The source being the beginning of the river.

For your house to sustain itself, it has to have a connection to the source. The pipes, which are our prayers, our praise, our purpose, keep us connected to the source, God himself. The pipes have a dual role. It brings the cleansing and fresh water, but also rids the house of the contaminated water. Prayers, praise, and purpose can get rid of contaminates that don't belong. Rid your home of waste that is generated just from living on this earth. I'm not going to go to much more into this, but just remember to keep your pipes functioning, so fresh water can come in and waste can go. You keep your pipes clean through obedience. 1 Samuel 15:22 in the message translation says, *"Then Samuel said, Do you think all GOD wants are sacrifices—empty rituals just for show? He wants you to listen to him! Plain listening is the thing, not staging a lavish religious production. Not doing what GOD tells you is far worse than fooling around in the occult."* God wants us to be obedient from start, rather than having to ask for forgiveness and repent because of disobedience.

The consequences of disobedience are worse than if we would have just obeyed. Have you ever had plumbing problems such as a drain clogged, air in your water line, or septic tank backed-up? It's far more costly to fix a problem (disobedience) than if we would have done some routine maintenance to prevent the problem (obedience) to keep the proper flow going. Do you see, at this point, how the entire house is built on God, from staking the lot to rough-in the plumbing. It's no longer just about the foundation, but the entire house. The next step is framing. Framing is building the house to a weather-tight stage. We want to be able to finish construction on the house without worrying about the weather.

What elements are you fighting against? What are you trying to keep out your life? Our framing is the armor of God. Ephesians 6:11-18 says, *"11 Put on the whole armour of God, that ye may be able to stand against the wiles of the devil. 12 For we wrestle not against flesh and blood, but against principalities, against powers, against the rulers of the darkness of this world, against spiritual wickedness in high places. 13 Wherefore take unto you the whole armour of God, that ye may be able to withstand in the evil day, and having done all, to stand. 14 Stand therefore, having your loins girt about with truth, and having on the breastplate of righteousness; 15 And your feet shod with the preparation of the gospel of peace; 16 Above all, taking the shield of faith, wherewith ye shall be able to quench all the fiery darts of the wicked .17 And take the helmet of salvation, and the sword of the Spirit, which is the word of God: 18 Praying always with all prayer and supplication in the Spirit, and watching thereunto with all perseverance and supplication for all saints;"* 2 Corinthians 2:11, *"Lest Satan should get an advantage of us: for we are not ignorant of his devices."* We have to frame the home to keep Satan out. With the armor of God, we have the entire home covered.

We've even tapped below the home to the source, which keeps the home operable. We have built this home to withstand whatever storms the devil brings our way. We can add the exterior next. What are you going to look like? Are you an overcomer? Are you victorious? Do you walk around looking defeated? Do you look as if you have no hope? John 16:33, *"These things I have spoken unto you, that in me ye might have* peace. *In the world ye shall have tribulation: but be of good cheer; I have overcome the world."* Psalms 41:11, *"By this I know that thou favourest me, because mine enemy doth not triumph over me."* 2 Corinthians 2:14 says, *"Now thanks be unto God, which always causeth us to triumph in Christ, and maketh manifest the savour of his knowledge by us in every place."* 1 Corinthians 15:57, *"But thanks be to God, which giveth us the victory through our Lord Jesus Christ.* 1 John 5:4, *"For whatsoever is born of God overcometh the world: and this is the victory that overcometh the world, even our faith."* These scriptures tell us how we should look. We should look victorious, triumphant, and authoritative. The devil has already been defeated.

Our hope is in God. Psalms 42:11 says, *"Why art thou cast down, O my soul? and why art thou disquieted within me? hope thou in God: for I shall yet praise him, who is the health of my countenance, and my God."* Lamentations 3:24, *"Lord is my portion, saith my soul; therefore will I hope in him."* 1 Peter 1:21 says, *"Who by him do believe in God, that raised him up from the dead, and gave him glory; that your faith and hope might be in God."* Your exterior should show your uniqueness. Psalms 139:14 in the amplified says, *"I will give thanks and praise to You, for I am fearfully and wonderfully made; Wonderful are Your works, And my soul knows it very well."* Your exterior should show your spiritual gift.

1 Corinthians 12:4-12 talks about the spiritual gifts. The Bible says, *"4 Now there are diversities of gifts, but the same Spirit. 5 And there are differences of administrations, but the same Lord. 6 And there are diversities of operations, but it is the same God which worketh all in all. 7 But the manifestation of the Spirit is given to every man to profit withal. 8 For to one is given by the Spirit the word of wisdom; to another the word of knowledge by*

the same Spirit; *9 To another faith by the same Spirit; to another the gifts of healing by the same Spirit; 10 To another the working of miracles; to another prophecy; to another discerning of spirits; to another divers kinds of tongues; to another the interpretation of tongues: 11 But all these worketh that one and the selfsame Spirit, dividing to every man severally as he will. 12 For as the body is one, and hath many members, and all the members of that one body, being many, are one body: so also is Christ."* The steps to building the homes are the same, but when it comes to the exterior, you can show your differences.

Now, the neighborhood works together for the upkeep of the homes within the neighborhood. There are other steps in building a house, but the next and last step I want to discuss is the roofing. The roofing process consists of sheathing, flashing, shingling, and the ridge caps. The roofing process is added protection from moisture to the home. The roof covers every area of the home. Your covering is the blood of Jesus. It covers every area of your life. The blood of Jesus purifies, pardons, and protects. 1 John 1:7 says, *"But if we walk in the light, as he is in the light, we have fellowship one with another, and the blood of Jesus Christ his Son cleanseth us from all sin."* Romans 3: 23-26, *"23 For all have sinned, and come short of the glory of God; 24 Being justified freely by his grace through the redemption that is in Christ Jesus: 25 Whom God hath set forth to be a propitiation through faith in his blood, to declare his righteousness for the remission of sins that are past, through the forbearance of God; 26 To declare, I say, at this time his righteousness: that he might be just, and the justifier of him which believeth in Jesus."* Hebrews 10:16-22, *"16 This is the covenant that I will make with them after those days, saith the Lord, I will put my laws into their hearts, and in their minds will I write them; 17 And their sins and iniquities will*

I remember no more. ¹⁸ Now where remission of these is, there is no more offering for sin. ¹⁹ Having therefore, brethren, boldness to enter into the holiest by the blood of Jesus, ²⁰ By a new and living way, which he hath consecrated for us, through the veil, that is to say, his flesh; ²¹ And having an high priest over the house of God; ²² Let us draw near with a true heart in full assurance of faith, having our hearts sprinkled from an evil conscience, and our bodies washed with pure water. ²³ Let us hold fast the profession of our faith without wavering; (for he is faithful that promised;)." As you can see in scriptures, we have been purified and pardoned.

In Exodus 12:13, *"And the blood shall be to you for a token upon the houses where ye are: and when I see the blood, I will pass over you, and the plague shall not be upon you to destroy you, when I smite the land of Egypt."* When your house is covered by the blood, the devil and his demons have to pass over. You are protected from harm and danger. Remember to always apply the blood and plea the blood to keep that protection. When you don't apply the blood, you get leaks in your roof. All the devil needs is a small opening to get into the house. Then before you know it, he has opened the door and invited in his cronies. Now the house is inhabited by things that could destroy it such as mold, rot, termites, and other pests. In other words, envy, jealousy, hate, or any works of the flesh. Keep the house standing by building it on the rock, our savior, which is Jesus the Christ.

Being Virtuous: A Virtuous Woman
Foundational Text: Ruth 3:11

"And now, my daughter, do not fear. I will do for you all that you request, for all the people of my town know that you are a virtuous woman."

We all know Proverbs 31 when it comes to talking about a virtuous woman, but I want to look at a virtuous woman from the example of Ruth. Our foundational text tells us that Ruth is a virtuous woman. The words of Boaz, before he became her husband, says, *"And now, my daughter, do not fear. I will do for you all that you request, for all the people of my town know that you are a virtuous woman."* We hear women all the time who want to be married say that I am looking for my Boaz. I want a Boaz. I know there is a Boaz out there for me. My question to you is, "Are you a Ruth?" Do you possess the attributes of a virtuous woman? Are you displaying or exhibiting the character of a virtuous woman? Let us look at what it means to be a virtuous woman and why did Boaz call Ruth a virtuous woman. According to the dictionary, to be virtuous is to be conforming to moral and ethical principles, morally excellent, upright, chaste. The Word defines virtuous even better, so go to Proverbs 31 so we can see the attributes of a virtuous woman; did Ruth have those attributes? Starting at verse 10, *"Who can find a virtuous wife? For her worth is far above rubies."* A virtuous woman is priceless. She cannot be bought. She has standards. She has self-worth and she knows that self-worth. Ruth 2:1-3 says, *"There was a relative of Naomi's husband, a man of great wealth, of the family of Elimelech. His name was Boaz. ²So Ruth the Moabitess said to Naomi, "Please let me go to the field, and glean heads of grain after him in whose sight I may find favor." And she said to her, "Go, my daughter. "³Then she left, and went and gleaned in the field after the reapers. And she happened to come to the part of the field belonging to Boaz, who was of the family of Elimelech."*

She went to work. She said let me go to the field and glean heads of grain. To glean means to gather slowly and laboriously, bit by bit. She was not lazy. She put in work, so she could find favor from the owner. What do you do at your job to get your boss's attention so you can get that raise or promotion? Are you putting in the work, or do you just expect a raise because you've been on the job for years and feel the company owes it to you when you really are not producing? Ruth put in the work and knew her worth. Verse 11, in Proverbs 31, *"The heart of her husband safely trusts her; So he will have no lack of gain."* Are you trustworthy, or just after that man so you can get your hands on what he has? Can he talk to you about anything without judgement and condemnation? Has he seen the real you, or the one you are showing him just to get him?

Ruth 2 continues, *"⁵Then Boaz said to his servant who was in charge of the reapers, "Whose young woman is this?" ⁶So the servant who was in charge of the reapers answered and said, "It is the young Moabite woman who came back with Naomi from the country of Moab. ⁷And she said, 'Please let me glean and gather after the reapers among the sheaves.' So she came and has continued from morning until now, though she rested a little in the house." ⁸Then Boaz said to Ruth, "You will listen, my daughter, will you not? Do not go to glean in another field, nor go from here, but* stay close by my young women. ⁹ Let your eyes be on the field which they reap and go after them. Have I not commanded the young men not to touch you? And when you are thirsty, go to the vessels and drink from what the young men have drawn." ¹⁰ So she fell on her face, bowed down to the ground, and said to him, "Why have I found favor in your eyes, that you should take notice of me, since I am a foreigner?" ¹¹ And Boaz answered and said to her, "It has been fully reported to me, all that you have done for your mother-in-law since the death of your husband, and how you have left your father and your mother and the land of your birth, and have come to a people whom you did not know before. ¹² The LORD repay your work, and a full reward be given you by the LORD God of Israel, under whose wings you have come for refuge." ¹³ Then she said, "Let me find favor in your sight, my lord; for you have comforted me, and have spoken [a]kindly to your maidservant, though I am not like one of your maidservants." ¹⁴ Now Boaz said to her at mealtime, "Come here, and eat of the bread, and dip your piece of bread in the vinegar." So she sat beside the reapers, and he passed parched grain to her; and she ate and was satisfied, and kept some back. ¹⁵ And when she rose up to [b]glean, Boaz commanded his young men, saying, "Let her glean even among the sheaves, and do not [c]reproach her. ¹⁶ Also let grain from the bundles fall purposely for her; leave it that she may glean, and do not rebuke her." ¹⁷ So she gleaned in the field until evening, and beat out what she had gleaned, and it was about an ephah of barley. ¹⁸ Then she took it up and went into the city, and her mother-in-law saw what she had gleaned. So she brought out and gave to her what she had kept back after she had been satisfied. ¹⁹ And her mother-in-law said to her, "Where have you gleaned today? And where did you work? Blessed be the one who took notice of you.

"So she told her mother-in-law with whom she had worked, and said, "The man's name with whom I worked today is Boaz." **20** *Then Naomi said to her daughter-in-law, "Blessed be he of the LORD, who has not forsaken His kindness to the living and the dead!" And Naomi said to her, "This man is a relation of ours, one of [d]our close relatives."* **21** *Ruth the Moabitess said, "He also said to me, 'You shall stay close by my young men until they have finished all my harvest.' "* **22** *And Naomi said to Ruth her daughter-in-law, "It is good, my daughter, that you go out with his young women, and that people do not [e]meet you in any other field."* **23** *So she stayed close by the young women of Boaz, to glean until the end of barley harvest and wheat harvest; and she dwelt with her mother-in-law."*

Boaz has a conversation with Ruth, and in that conversation, he sees her humility, her willingness to be obedient, submissive, her willingness to separate from family, and her thankfulness. He has heard of her reputation. He sees that she fears the Lord. I used the word sees because it is not just about what your mouth says, but what does your action say? Your words must line up with the word. You cannot say one thing, and then your actions do not reflect what you have said. Trust is lost, if there ever was any. Now Boaz has noticed Ruth just by the work she does and how she carries herself. Boaz decides to take it further. The company has a luncheon. Let me observe how she is in public around other people, how she is with her co-workers. Are you at the table being loud, gossiping, complaining, gluttonous, and without table manners? Ruth could not eat all the food; she got a to-go plate for what she did not eat. She then went back to work and got right back to her assignment. She took home her paycheck and leftovers from the luncheon to take care of her family, which was Naomi.

She tells Naomi about her day, which included meeting Boaz and the luncheon. Women, you know how we get when we think we have a man's attention and want him to pursue us. In the next chapter of Ruth, Ruth further gets Boaz's attention without compromising herself.

Ruth 3:1-5, *"Then Naomi her mother-in-law said to her, "My daughter, shall I not seek security[a] for you, that it may be well with you? ² Now Boaz, whose young women you were with, is he not our relative? In fact, he is winnowing barley tonight at the threshing floor. ³ Therefore wash yourself and anoint yourself, put on your best garment and go down to the threshing floor; but do not make yourself known to the man until he has finished eating and drinking. ⁴ Then it shall be, when he lies down, that you shall notice the place where he lies; and you shall go in, uncover his feet, and lie down; and he will tell you what you should do." ⁵ And she said to her, "All that you say to me I will do."* There is a party, and Boaz is attending. Now ladies, you know how we do it, but many of us do it wrong. You do not have to go to a party dressed like a harlot, showing everyone what you have to offer. You do not have to go with everything being fake. Be confident in your self-image and love yourself as you are. Have self-esteem that gives you boldness in who you are. The men are not trying to hide their guts, jacked-up teeth, or receding hairline. You either take it or leave it. They walk up boldly to you and smile with that missing tooth. No offense to the men. Just making a point that we women need to be real with ourselves so we can real with the men. Now Ruth does what Naomi says and ends up getting some alone time with Boaz. It gets late in the night, but they have a chance to talk. All they did was talk. Ruth puts her cards on the table and wants marriage. Ladies, if you want marriage, be bold enough to let the man know that is what you want and that is what you want to work towards. If he does not want the same thing, then he is not the one God has for you and there is no point in the two of you wasting one another's time.

Go back to Proverbs 31 and we will pick it up in verse 12, *"She does him good and not evil All the days of her life. 13 She seeks wool and flax, And willingly works with her hands. 14 She is like the merchant ships, She brings her food from afar. 15 She also rises while it is yet night, And provides food for her household, And a portion for her maidservants. She considers a field and buys it; From [e]her profits she plants a vineyard. 17 She girds herself with strength, And strengthens her arms. 18 She perceives that her merchandise is good, her lamp does not go out by night. 19 She stretches out her hands to the distaff, And her hand holds the spindle. 20 She extends her hand to the poor, Yes, she reaches out her hands to the needy. 21 She is not afraid of snow for her household, For all her household is clothed with scarlet. 22 She makes tapestry for herself; Her clothing is fine linen and purple. 23 Her husband is known in the gates, When he sits among the elders of the land. 24 She makes linen garments and sells them, And supplies sashes for the merchants. 25 Strength and honor are her clothing; She shall rejoice in time to come. 26 She opens her mouth with wisdom, And on her tongue is the law of kindness. 27 She watches over the ways of her household, And does not eat the bread of idleness. 28 Her children rise up and call her blessed; Her husband also, and he praises her: 29 "Many daughters have done well, But you excel them all."* ³⁰ *Charm is deceitful and beauty is passing, But a woman who fears the* LORD, *she shall be praised.* ³¹ *Give her of the fruit of her hands, And let her own works praise her in the gates."*

Proverbs 31 talks about being a virtuous wife, but I submit to you that you first must be a virtuous woman in order to be a virtuous wife. Ruth was a virtuous woman, so it was easy to carry that virtuousness into her role as wife. Boaz saw in Ruth what he wanted as his wife, and he did what was necessary to make her his wife. Back in Ruth, chapter 4, it says, *"Now Boaz went up to the gate and sat down there; and behold, the close relative of whom Boaz had spoken came by. So Boaz said, "Come aside,* [a]*friend, sit down here." So he came aside and sat down.* ² *And he took ten men of the elders of the city, and said, "Sit down here." So they sat down.* ³ *Then he said to the close relative, "Naomi, who has come back from the country of Moab, sold the piece of land which belonged to our brother Elimelech.* ⁴ *And I thought to* [b]*inform you, saying, 'Buy it back in the presence of the inhabitants and the elders of my people. If you will redeem it, redeem it; but if* [c]*you will not redeem it, then tell me, that I may know; for there is no one but you to redeem it, and I am next after you.' "And he said, "I will redeem it."* ⁵ *Then Boaz said, "On the day you buy the field from the hand of Naomi, you must also buy it from Ruth the Moabitess, the wife of the dead, to* [d]*perpetuate the name of the dead through his inheritance."* ⁶ *And the close relative said, "I cannot redeem it for myself, lest I ruin my own inheritance. You redeem my right of redemption for yourself, for I cannot redeem it."* ⁷ *Now this was the custom in former times in Israel concerning redeeming and exchanging, to confirm anything: one man took off his sandal and*

gave it to the other, and this was a confirmation in Israel.
⁸ Therefore the close relative said to Boaz, "Buy it for yourself." So
he took off his sandal. ⁹ And Boaz said to the elders and all the
people, "You are witnesses this day that I have bought all that was
Elimelech's, and all that was Chilion's and Mahlon's, from the hand
of Naomi. ¹⁰ Moreover, Ruth the Moabitess, the widow of Mahlon, I
have acquired as my wife, to perpetuate the name of the dead
through his inheritance, that the name of the dead may not be cut
off from among his brethren and from [ᵍ]his position at the gate.
You are witnesses this day." ¹¹ And all the people who were at the
gate, and the elders, said, "We are witnesses. The LORD make the
woman who is coming to your house like Rachel and Leah, the two
who built the house of Israel; and may you prosper in Ephrathah
and be famous in Bethlehem. ¹² May your house be like the house
of Perez, whom Tamar bore to Judah, because of the offspring
which the LORD will give you from this young woman." Boaz
followed the customs of the day and took the steps necessary to
make Ruth his wife. Look at it and what it is. *⁹ And Boaz said to*
the elders and all the people, "You are witnesses this day that I
have bought all that was Elimelech's, and all that was Chilion's
and Mahlon's, from the hand of Naomi. ¹⁰ Moreover, Ruth the
Moabitess, the widow of Mahlon, I have acquired as my wife, to
perpetuate the name of the dead through his inheritance, that the
name of the dead may not be cut off from among his brethren and
from [ᵍ]his position at the gate." Look at God. The devil thought
he had you. Your husband died, you have no children, you have
no money, you lost your job, you lost your benefits, there is no
insurance policy, you have mounting bills and debts, BUT GOD.
Boaz bought all that was Mahlon's, Ruth's dead husband, from
Naomi to make Ruth his wife.

Not only did Ruth get who and what she wanted, but Naomi and her family got blessed as well. Ruth got restored to her what she thought she lost. Your blessing may not come in the way you expect it, but it will still come. Verse 13 continues to say, *"13 So Boaz took Ruth and she became his wife; and when he went in to her, the LORD gave her conception, and she bore a son. 14 Then the women said to Naomi, "Blessed be the LORD, who has not left you this day without a [f]close relative; and may his name be famous in Israel! 15 And may he be to you a restorer of life and a [g]nourisher of your old age; for your daughter-in-law, who loves you, who is better to you than seven sons, has borne him." 16 Then Naomi took the child and laid him on her bosom, and became a nurse to him. 17 Also the neighbor women gave him a name, saying, "There is a son born to Naomi." And they called his name Obed. He is the father of Jesse, the father of David."* Ruth and Boaz continued to bless Naomi and gave her their son, who is in the genealogy of Jesus.

I say all of this to say first to the single ladies, be virtuous now as you patiently await to become a wife. You only must walk uprightly, and God will turn the head of the man who is to become your husband. He will notice you by the way you carry yourself, your conversation, and by your moral and ethical principles. He will notice you by your character. If you are already married and you are not carrying yourself as a virtuous woman, it is not too late. You first need to repent of your sins.

Ask God to forgive you and cleanse you of all unrighteousness. Then ask your husband to forgive. Let him know you want to be his crown and you no longer want to be a cancer in his life. Proverbs 12:4 states, *"A virtuous woman is a crown to her husband: but she that maketh ashamed is as rottenness in his bones."* You need to confess that you are a virtuous woman, and your husband and children call you blessed. Continually apply the blood of Jesus to those areas in your life that lead you to unrighteousness, that cause you to stumble, that cause you to fail the tests. Praise God in advance for changing your character and erasing your past mistakes from the minds of people who would always remind you of your mistakes and hold them against you.

As you become the woman or wife described in Proverbs 31, there are several principles that we need to understand and take from the scripture. Let us first read Proverbs 31:10-31 in The Message translation, *"A good woman is hard to find, and worth far more than diamonds. Her husband trusts her without reserve, and never has reason to regret it. Never spiteful, she treats him generously all her life long. She shops around for the best yarns and cottons, and enjoys knitting and sewing. She's like a trading ship that sails to faraway places and brings back exotic surprises. She's up before dawn, preparing breakfast for her family and organizing her day. She looks over a field and buys it, then, with money she's put aside, plants a garden. First thing in the morning, she dresses for work, rolls up her sleeves, eager to get started. She senses the worth of her work, is in no hurry to call it quits for the day. She's skilled in the crafts of home and hearth, diligent in homemaking. She's quick to assist anyone in need, reaches out to help the poor. She doesn't worry about her family when it snows; their winter clothes are all mended and ready to wear. She makes her own clothing, and dresses in colorful linens and silks. Her husband is greatly respected when he deliberates with the city fathers. She designs gowns and sells them, brings the sweaters she knits to the dress shops. Her clothes are well-made and elegant, and she always faces tomorrow with a smile. When she speaks she has something worthwhile to say, and she always says it kindly. She keeps an eye on everyone in her household, and keeps them all busy and productive. Her children respect and bless her; her husband joins in with words of praise: "Many women have done wonderful things, but you've outclassed them all!" Charm can mislead and beauty soon fades. The woman to be admired and praised is the woman who lives in the Fear-of-God. Give her everything she deserves! Adorn her life with praises!"*

The principle is Partnership. The wife is to be the husband's helpmeet. Genesis 2:18 says, *"And the Lord God said, It is not good that the man should be alone; I will make him an help meet for him."* The wife always has her husband's best interests, and the husband does not regret making her his wife. She takes good care of him. The wife works, not only in the home but outside the home. She brings income to the household and makes investments that will benefit the household. Her husband praises her for all that she does and who she is.

The next principle is Preparation. She is organized and prepares for her day. She gets things ready for her family, then she gets ready for her day and all that it may bring. She is prepared to put in the work. There is the principle of Productivity. She produces and makes sure her children produce. She keeps her children busy. She stays busy but all to produce for her household. She makes sure that everyone is taken care of and all their needs are met. She has the skills to get the work done whether it is cooking, planting, sewing, selling, or homemaking. She is productive. She is a successful businesswoman. The Bible shows that you can have a career and family. We must keep a balance between career and family. The issues arise when there is not a balance, and we are not doing God's will but our own. That leads me to my final principle of Purpose.

The wife in Proverbs 31 is walking in and living out her purpose. When you are following the will of God for your life, you do not live in your own strength but his strength. This wife gets up early, gets things together for her family, goes to work and works late, and still makes sure her household is functioning as it should, and she does it all it a smile. Only in God's strength because I got tired just thinking about it. When you are living out your purpose, you are blessed in the city, blessed in fields, blessed when you come, and blessed when you go. You will be praised and admired by all you come into contact with. You will give God the glory and praise for all he has done, all he is doing, and all he is going to do in your life. It is all because you fear the Lord. Live on Purpose!!!

Fear Not and Fear Not

Foundational texts:

2 Timothy 1:7 *For God hath not given us the spirit of fear; but of power; and of love, and of a sound mind.*

Proverbs 1:7 *The fear of the Lord is the beginning of knowledge, but fools despise wisdom and instruction.*

We talk much about faith. Releasing our faith, building our faith, having the Godkind of faith, and using our faith. What I want to discuss is fear, which is the opposite of faith, and the power it has over us. As stated in the foundational text, God didn't give us a spirit of fear, and fear is a spirit. Ask yourselves where this spirit comes from and why do I allow it to have so much power over me. We know that all things that are not of God is of his adversary, the devil. The devil has so much power over us, and we have yet to realize it. We may only think of the devil using us when we're committing sins.

Ephesians 6: 11-12 says, *"Put on the whole armour of God that ye may be able to stand against the wiles of the devil. For we wrestle not against flesh and blood, but against principalities, against powers, against the rulers of the darkness of this world, against spiritual wickedness in high places."* As long as we're in this world, we will be wrestling with the darkness of this world, with spirits of wickedness such as fear. The wiles of the devil are whatever plans and strategies he can use to take you out the will of God. Your disobedience can take you out the will of God. Your failure to commit can take you out the will of God. Your failure to act can take you out the will of God. Your tongue can take you out the will of God. Proverbs 18:21 states that, *"Death and life are in the power of the tongue; and they that love it shall eat the fruit thereof".* You shall have whatever you are speaking. Many times, when we're in fear, we do nothing. We don't move backwards or forwards. We stand where we are in our comfort zones and ask God why nothing is happening in our lives, and God is saying look in the mirror. God will always do his part. When will we do ours?

1 John 4:18 says, *"There is no fear in love; but perfect love casteth out fear; because fear hath torment. He that feareth is not made perfect in love."* We know that God is love, so there is no fear in God. Since we are of God, there should be no fear in us. When we allow fear to have a grip on us, and fail to live out our purpose and fulfill the will of God, we're saying that we don't trust God and what His word says for us. We place our trust in the doctors and medicine, in lawyers and the law, in jobs and that paycheck. If you went to see a doctor and he gave you bad news, would you trust that God has already healed you because He is Jehovah Rapha? Isaiah 53:5 states, *"But he was wounded for our transgressions, he was bruised for our iniquities: the chastisement of our peace was upon him; and with his stripes we are healed".*

Do you claim your healing and praise Him in advance, or do you live in fear in what is to come? When we're faced with challenges involving the legislation and the court system, do we trust God to see us through, or do we place our trust in the lawyers? 1 John 5:4 says, "For whatsoever is born of God overcometh the world: and this is the victory that overcometh the world, even our faith." He is Jehovah Nissi, the Lord God our victory. If you lose your job, do you trust that God will make a way, or will you turn to iniquity until you get another job? He is Jehovah Jireh, our provider. Why do we fear? Genesis 1:26 says, *"And God said, Let us make man in our image, after our likeness: and let them have dominion over the fish of the sea, and over the fowl of the air, and over the cattle, and over all the earth, and over every creeping thing that creepeth upon the earth."* We are to have dominion over all the earth. Dominion is sovereign authority.

We fear because we fail to realize who we are in Christ Jesus and that Jesus restored us to a place of having dominion and power. In Ephesians chapter 1, Paul is talking to the people of Ephesus and he says in the amplified version of verses 17-19, *"17 [I always pray] that the God of our Lord Jesus Christ, the Father of glory, may grant you a spirit of wisdom and of revelation [that gives you a deep and personal and intimate insight] into the true knowledge of Him [for we know the Father through the Son]. 18 And [I pray] that the eyes of your heart [the very center and core of your being] may be enlightened [flooded with light by the Holy Spirit], so that you will know and cherish the [f]hope [the divine guarantee, the confident expectation] to which He has called you, the riches of His glorious inheritance in the [g]saints (God's people), 19 and [so that you will begin to know] what the immeasurable and unlimited and surpassing greatness of His [active, spiritual] power is in us who believe."*

We need a revelation of who He is, so we know who we are in Him. The spirit of fear is so powerful, God must tell us that it didn't come from him. God tells us to fear not, over and over. Isaiah 41:10 says, *"Fear thou not; for I am with thee: be not* dismayed; for I am thy God: I will strengthen thee; yea, I will help thee; yea, I will uphold thee with the right hand of my righteousness." Deuteronomy 31:6 says, "Be strong and of a good courage, fear not, nor be afraid of them: for the LORD thy God, he it is that doth go with thee; he will not fail thee, nor forsake thee." Hebrews 13:5-6 says, "Let your conversation be without covetousness; and be content with such things as ye have: for he hath said, I will never leave thee, nor forsake thee. 6 So that we may boldly say, The Lord is my helper, and I will not fear what man shall do unto me." Each time we see that the Lord is with us. Do we not believe that He is with us, that He would never leave nor forsake us?

When we look throughout the Bible, we see people in fear and God says fear not. Abraham was in fear, Moses was in fear, Joshua was in fear, Gideon was in fear, David was in fear, Elijah was in fear, the Widow Woman, even Jesus was in fear in the garden. Yet, they were obedient to the will of the Father. They acted and stood on God's word. They didn't let fear keep them from the promises of God. Jesus is our example on overcoming fear. When Jesus said nevertheless, not my will, but thy will be done, The Bible says, "And there appeared an angel unto him from heaven, strengthening him."

When you make that decision to action and not allow the spirit of fear to hold you back, you will be immediately strengthened so you can follow through on doing God's will. Hebrews 12:2 says, "Looking unto Jesus the author and finisher of our faith; who for the joy that was set before him endured the cross, despising the shame, and is set down at the right hand of the throne of God." When you know on the other side of fear is that manifested blessing you've been waiting for, the promise in your life you've been waiting to come to pass, the spirit of fear should flee, and the spirit of faith should be abounding. When you know without a shadow of doubt that God is with you, who or what can stand against you? When you look throughout God's word, you see how God delivers people out of fearful situations. He was with the three Hebrew boys in the fiery furnace. When the king looked in the furnace, he saw four, and they all came out. Daniel in the lion's den should have been attacked and eaten up by the lions, but he came out.

The Israelites fleeing from Pharaoh, crossing the Red Sea on dry land, and their captors drowning when the waters came back together. They came out. Jonah in the belly of the whale, but he came out. Joseph in the pit, but he came out. Jesus dying on the cross, defeating death, hell, and the grave, but He came out. When are you going to trust that God is with you, so you can come out. We see what can happen when we allow fear to take hold on us. The Israelites wandered in the wilderness for forty years. God had promised them the land. He was with them.

In Numbers 13, we see what can happen when we fear and doubt. Starting in verse 25, *"And they returned from searching of the land after forty days. 26 And they went and came to Moses, and to Aaron, and to all the congregation of the children of Israel, unto the wilderness of Paran, to Kadesh; and brought back word unto them, and unto all the congregation, and shewed them the fruit of the land. 27 And they told him, and said, We came unto the land whither thou sentest us, and surely it floweth with milk and honey; and this is the fruit of it. 28 Nevertheless the people be strong that dwell in the land, and the cities are walled, and very great: and moreover we saw the children of Anak there. 29 The Amalekites dwell in the land of the south: and the Hittites, and the Jebusites, and the Amorites, dwell in the mountains: and the Canaanites dwell by the sea, and by the coast of Jordan. 30 And*

Caleb stilled the people before Moses, and said, Let us go up at once, and possess it; for we are well able to overcome it. 31 But the men that went up with him said, We be not able to go up against the people; for they are stronger than we. 32 And they brought up an evil report of the land which they had searched unto the children of Israel, saying, The land, through which we have gone to search it, is a land that eateth up the inhabitants thereof; and all the people that we saw in it are men of a great stature. 33 And there we saw the giants, the sons of Anak, which come of the giants: and we were in our own sight as grasshoppers, and so we were in their sight."

How are you seeing yourself? What has God promised you that hasn't come to pass because of what you're seeing and experiencing in the natural? Many things in our lives are delayed because of our own doing and we blame God. We say he doesn't want to answer our prayers or honor our requests and petitions when he has already done both, but it has yet to manifest because of our disobedience due to fear. We say all the time that we're in faith, standing in faith, but are we? Faith requires action. The Bible says faith without works is dead. What are you doing to bring God's promises to pass in your life and the lives of others? Your fear of acting can be causing a delay in someone else's manifested blessings. It's not just about you.

God said fear not because you should fear not. The foundational text says, *"The fear of the Lord is the beginning of knowledge, but fools despise wisdom and instruction."* We function in a spirit of fear because we fear not the Lord. Fearing the Lord is reverencing who He is; it is not being scared or afraid of him. We have allowed the enemy to pervert who God is. We've turned God into him, and God said, don't call me the devil. There is so much confusion and we know the devil is the author of confusion. 1 Corinthians 14:33 says, *"For God is not the author of confusion, but of peace, as in all churches of the saints."* When things go wrong in our lives or are not going like we want them to go, we blame everyone, except ourselves. We blame God, the devil, other people, never wanting to look in the mirror. The Bible says in Hebrews 12:5-7, *"And ye have forgotten the exhortation which speaketh unto you as unto children, My son, despise not thou the chastening of the Lord, nor faint when thou art rebuked of him:6 For whom the Lord loveth he chasteneth, and scourgeth every son whom he receiveth.7 If ye endure chastening, God dealeth with you as with sons; for what son is he whom the father chasteneth not?"*

When we look at the definition of chastise, we see it means to discipline. God is our Father, and as our natural father disciplines us, so does our Heavenly Father. Have you ever allowed your child or children to go through some things, so they can learn a life lesson? Have you seen your child through some things that they needed to go through to learn for themselves? Have you warned your child about some friends or things and they didn't listen? Was your child ever disobedient and you disciplined them in some way? If you have, do they call you the devil? Or do they thank you for being there for them, and are they grateful later in life for the lesson?

So, it is with God. He allows us to go through some things, so we can learn who He is, so we can be a testament to others of who He is, so we can fear who He is. In the word discipline, which is another way of saying chastening, I see disciple. Discipline brings about discipleship through the fearing of the Lord. When we truly understand who God is, when we stop putting Him in a box and put Him in his rightful place, our lives will never be the same again. You can't be the same when you see him and know him to be your creator. You can't be the same when you see Him and know Him to be your Strong Tower. You can't be the same when you see Him and know Him to be your Savior, Redeemer, Justifier, Reconciler, and Sanctifier. You can't be the same when we see Him and know Him to be your Living Water and Bread of Life. You can't be the same when you see Him and know Him to be your Provider, Way Maker, Sustainer. You can't be the same when you see Him and know Him to be your Healer. You can't be the same when you see Him and know Him to be your Victory in all situations and circumstances. You can't be the same when you see Him and know Him to be your Prince of Peace. You can't be the same when you see Him and know Him to be Alpha and Omega. You can't be the same when you see and know Him to be the all-knowing, all-present, all-sufficient one. You can't be the same when you see and know Him to be the Everlasting God. You can't be the same when you see and know Him to be your Lord of Lords and King of Kings. You can't be the same when we see and know Him to be your All in All. When you know who he is, you can't help but to fear him.

Proverbs 19:23 says, *"The fear of the LORD tendeth to life: and he that hath it shall abide satisfied; he shall not be visited with evil."* 23:17 says, *"Let not thine heart envy sinners: but be thou in the fear of the LORD all the day long."* Revelations 15:4, *"Who shall not fear thee, O Lord, and glorify thy name? for thou only art holy: for all nations shall come and worship before thee; for thy judgments are made manifest."* Because we don't fear the Lord as we should, we place limits on him. He is a limitless God. Matthew 19:26, *"But Jesus beheld them, and said unto them, With men this is impossible; but with God all things are possible."* Mark says it this way in 9:23, *"Jesus said unto him, If thou canst believe, all things are possible to him that believeth."* Our problem is that we don't believe that God is able to do all things. We look at God as if he's one of us. We look at Him in this way because we have become a part of this world. Instead of just being in it, we're now of it. We don't even recognize who we are. We see the body, the material things of the world, the natural things of this world, and we have forgotten we are spiritual beings. This is all temporary.

2 Corinthians 4:18 tells us, *"While we look not at the things which are seen, but at the things which are not seen: for the things which are seen are temporal; but the things which are not seen are eternal."* We are so focused on the temporary things that we are allowing the eternal things to go by the wayside. We're on a path and destiny straight to an eternal fire if we don't wake up and get back to who we truly are, servants of the Most High God; get back to God through repentance, reverence, restoration, revelation, and transformation. God is waiting on us to fear not and to fear not.

Can we start today just praising God for who he is? Can we start just reverencing the name of Jesus? Can we start exalting and lifting up the name of Jesus? He's worthy to be praised. He's worthy to be exalted and adored. He's worthy to be glorified. God, I just want to thank you for who you are. I want to thank you for being a merciful God. I want to thank you for being a gracious God. I want to thank you for being a Holy God. Thank you for being a loving God. There is none like you. You are an Almighty God. You are a Great God. You are an Amazing God. You are an Awesome God. There is none like you, O God. I just thank you and praise you for who you are. I just love you, O God. I just thank you and praise you for loving me when I didn't love myself. Thank you for always being there for me, for keeping me and protecting me. Thank you for cleansing me. Thank you for saving me. Thank you for your wisdom and revelations. Thank you for your Holy Spirit who is my teacher, guide, and comforter. Thank you for peace that surpassed all understanding. Thank you for shedding your blood that covers me. Thank you for your angels that are encamped around and about me. Thank you for life, health, and strength. Thank you for family and friends. Thank you for the many manifested blessings in my life. I thank you Lord that the lives of your people are being changed and transformed. I thank you that the scales are falling off their eyes, and they have ears to hear and hearts open to receive your word. I thank you Lord that more of your people are becoming doers of the word and are obedient to your voice. A stranger's voice they will not follow. I thank you that we are your sheep and you are our shepherd. I thank you and praise you in advance for what you're doing and what you're going to do in my life and in the lives of your people. In Jesus' Name, Amen.

Dead, Dry Places
Foundational Text: Ezekiel 37:1-6

"The hand of the LORD was upon me, and carried me out in the spirit of the LORD, and set me down in the midst of the valley which was full of bones, ² And caused me to pass by them round about: and, behold, there were very many in the open valley; and, lo, they were very dry. ³ And he said unto me, Son of man, can these bones live? And I answered, O Lord GOD, thou knowest. ⁴ Again he said unto me, Prophesy upon these bones, and say unto them, O ye dry bones, hear the word of the LORD. ⁵ Thus saith the Lord GOD unto these bones; Behold, I will cause breath to enter into you, and ye shall live: ⁶ And I will lay sinews upon you, and will bring up flesh upon you, and cover you with skin, and put breath in you, and ye shall live; and ye shall know that I am the LORD."

Living your life, going through the motions from day to day. Same routine daily, weekly, and then you look around and ask where did the time go? You reflect upon your life and determine that it's a valley full of dry bones. There are some dead places in your life that need restoring and resurrecting. There is no fruit of the spirit. Galatians 5:22-23 says, *"But the fruit of the Spirit is love, joy, peace, longsuffering, gentleness, goodness, faith, Meekness, temperance: against such there is no law."* I like how the message translation says it. *"But what happens when we live God's way? He brings gifts into our lives, much the same way that fruit appears in an orchard—things like affection for others, exuberance about life, serenity. We develop a willingness to stick with things, a sense of compassion in the heart, and a conviction that a basic holiness permeates things and people. We find ourselves involved in loyal commitments, not needing to force our way in life, able to marshal and direct our energies wisely. Legalism is helpless in bringing this about; it only gets in the way."* Have you become that selfish person that is only concerned about your own wants and needs? Are you depressed about life because things haven't gone according to your plans? Do you start a project or task and never complete it before moving on to something else? Do you lack sympathy and empathy for others? Are you judgmental of others?

If you have answered yes to any of these questions, then we have some dead, dry places in our lives and we need to restore the fruit of the spirit in those areas. We must first recognize and be convicted of the fact that we have these dead, dry places in the fruit of the spirit. Secondly, we must want the dead, dry places to live again and produce. Next, we must repent, forgive, and ask God to forgive us. Matthew 6:14-15, "For *if ye forgive men their trespasses, your heavenly Father will also forgive you:* 15 *But if ye forgive not men their trespasses, neither will your Father forgive your trespasses."* The dead, dry places will not come alive again when there is unforgiveness in your heart.

We must then speak to those dead, dry places. In speaking to those places, this consists of praying, worshipping, and confessing. Mark 11:23-26 says, *"For verily I say unto you, That whosoever shall say unto this mountain, Be thou removed, and be thou cast into the sea; and shall not doubt in his heart, but shall believe that those things which he saith shall come to pass; he shall have whatsoever he saith.* 24 *Therefore I say unto you, What things soever ye desire, when ye pray, believe that ye receive them, and ye shall have them.* 25 *And when ye stand praying, forgive, if ye have ought against any: that your Father also which is in heaven may forgive you your trespasses. ²⁶ But if ye do not forgive, neither will your Father which is in heaven forgive your trespasses."* Once again, we see the importance of forgiveness in restoring dead, dry places in our lives and being able to produce fruit. Psalms 146:1-2 says, *"Praise ye the LORD. Praise the LORD, O my soul. ² While I live will I praise the LORD: I will sing praises unto my God while I have any being."* Worship God. David says, "Praise the Lord, O my soul." Remember Psalms 23:3. He restores my soul. As worship takes place, the soul is getting involved. My mind, my will, my imagination, my emotions, and my intellect want to worship. My soul is becoming alive to God again.

Restoration is starting to take place. But listen, we can't stop at worship. We have to confess and speak to those dead, dry places. Talk to that fruit and tell it that you will produce again. I will have joy. I will have peace. I will grow and increase my faith. I am loved. I will show and give love. I will endure and run this race looking unto Jesus. I will be gentle in my actions and words. I am good, and I will do good. I am meek, humbly patient, and ready to be taught. I have self-control. As you continue to speak that fruit, the manifestation of restoration will show itself mighty and the fruit of the spirit will overflow. With the overflow of fruitfulness, you will be able to be a witness and a testament to others of how to rid their lives of the valley of dead, dry places.

What's Clogging Your Life
C. L. O. G.

Constraining Limits on God

Foundational Texts:

Acts 4:29 *"And now, Lord, behold their threatenings: and grant unto thy servants, that with all boldness they may speak thy word,"*

Isaiah 58:1-12 *"Cry aloud, spare not, lift up thy voice like a trumpet, and shew my people their transgression, and the house of Jacob their sins. ² Yet they seek me daily, and delight to know my ways, as a nation that did righteousness, and forsook not the ordinance of their God: they ask of me the ordinances of justice; they take delight in approaching to God. ³ Wherefore have we fasted, say they, and thou seest not? wherefore have we afflicted our soul, and thou takest no knowledge? Behold, in the day of your fast ye find pleasure, and exact all your labours. ⁴ Behold, ye fast for strife and debate, and to smite with the fist of wickedness: ye shall not fast as ye do this day, to make your voice to be heard on high. ⁵ Is it such a fast that I have chosen? a day for a man to afflict his soul? is it to bow down his head as a bulrush, and to spread sackcloth and ashes under him? wilt thou call this a fast, and an acceptable day to the LORD? ⁶ Is not this the fast that I have chosen? to loose the bands of wickedness, to undo the heavy burdens, and to let the oppressed go free, and that ye break every yoke? ⁷ Is it not to deal thy bread to the hungry, and that thou bring the poor that are cast out to thy house? when thou seest the naked, that thou cover him; and that thou hide not thyself from thine own flesh? ⁸ Then shall thy light break forth as the morning, and thine health shall spring forth speedily: and thy righteousness* *shall go before thee; the glory of the* L ORD *shall be thy reward.* 9 *Then shalt thou call, and the* L ORD *shall answer; thou shalt cry, and he shall say, Here I am. If thou take away from the midst of thee the yoke, the putting forth of the finger, and speaking vanity;* 10 *And if thou draw out thy soul to the hungry, and satisfy the afflicted soul; then shall thy light rise in obscurity, and thy darkness be as the noon day:* 11 *And the* L ORD *shall guide thee continually, and satisfy thy soul in drought, and make fat thy bones: and thou shalt be like a watered garden, and like a spring of water, whose waters fail not.* 12 *And they that shall be of thee shall build the old waste places: thou shalt raise up the foundations of many generations; and thou shalt be called, The repairer of the breach, The restorer of paths to dwell in."*

Recently, I had a problem with a sink in a bathroom. The problem hadn't existed for a while, so I thought it was fixed. Cut the water on and it runs, goes down the drain, and it's all clear, so it appears. There is no water standing in the sink, nothing. Go back later, the water has come back up, overflowing onto the floor; and get this, it's just as clear as when it went down. Clean the water up, put some drain cleaner down the drain, plunge it, snake it, run the water again, and problem fixed, right. Go back hours later and there's the water again as before. Repeat the process, but this time don't run the water for fear of it happening again. Is the problem fixed? Probably not. Don't know until I run the water again. Before running the water again, there should be a few things done.

A few examples would be shining a light down the drain to see if there is anything visible, taking the pipes apart and cleaning them out, or finding a cleanout in the waste line and feeding an auger through it if there are piping connections to other fixtures. Many times, in life, things happen in our life that occur in the natural that are parallel to what's occurring in the spiritual. Let's breakdown this problem that's happening in the natural to the problem that's happening in the spiritual. First thing, no recognition of a problem because that resource hasn't been used in a long time. Are you going about your life daily without using the resources that are available? Are you on autopilot because you're doing things on a routine basis, in your own world, in your own comfort zone?

John 3:16 says, *"For God so loved the world, that he gave his only begotten Son, that whosoever believeth in him should not perish, but have everlasting life."* We are perishing because we don't use our resources. We say we believe, but do we really believe? Do we live our life like we believe in him, or do we have a CLOG in our beliefs? Romans 10:8-13, *"But what saith it? The word is nigh thee, even in thy mouth, and in thy heart: that is, the word of faith, which we preach; 9 That if thou shalt confess with thy mouth the Lord Jesus, and shalt believe in thine heart that God hath raised him from the dead, thou shalt be saved. 10 For with the heart man believeth unto righteousness; and with the mouth confession is made unto salvation. 11 For the scripture saith, Whosoever believeth on him shall not be ashamed. 12 For there is no difference between the Jew and the Greek: for the same Lord over all is rich unto all that call upon him. 13 For whosoever shall call upon the name of the Lord shall be saved."* Your salvation is a resource. It entitles you to the entire Kingdom of God.

Matthew 6:33 states, *"But seek ye first the kingdom of God, and his righteousness; and all these things shall be added unto you."* We still have the issue of recognizing there is a problem because our salvation is only seen as getting us into heaven when it's so much more than just an entrance into the gates. When we said we wanted to be saved, ask yourselves did you really make him Lord? The answer would be a resounding no because we still want to be in control, do things our way, and be selfish. It's only when our way takes us in the wrong direction do we remember, oh, I have a resource I haven't used in a while, so let me call on the name of Jesus to fix it for me. Guess what, you have a CLOG. The water is running. You know the word. It's going down, but's there's a blockage you didn't even know existed because of no use of the resource. The water couldn't flow where it could reach your mind and heart.

Hebrews 8:10, *"For this is the covenant that I will make with the house of Israel after those days, saith the Lord; I will put my laws into their mind, and write them in their hearts: and I will be to them a God, and they shall be to me a people."* We still lack recognition because the water hasn't made its way back up to where it's visible. There's no realization that we're able to get to our covenant rights. We think everything is good. We go to service on Sundays, sometimes bible study during the week, pray every now and then, listen to a little gospel music occasionally, pay tithes, give occasional offerings, show compassion, and do other things you believe makes you a good servant. While doing those things, ask yourself again, why are you doing them and who are you really serving when doing them? My answer would be yourself.

There's still a lack of recognition that it's still about you and there is a CLOG. 1 Corinthians 3:18 says, *"Let no man deceive himself. If any man among you seemeth to be wise in this world, let him become a fool, that he may be wise."* We're deceiving ourselves into believing that we're serving God in ways that are pleasing to Him. 1 Peter 5:8, *"Be sober, be vigilant; because your adversary the devil, as a roaring lion, walketh about, seeking whom he may devour."* We haven't been vigilant because we've been devoured by the spirit of deception, and we failed to recognize it. Proverbs 28:1 is key. It says, *"The wicked flee when no man pursueth: but the righteous are bold as a lion."* The devil comes as a roaring lion, and we are to be as bold as a lion. Have you ever seen two lions fight? One lion is trying to take over the other's territory, and they get into a fight for that territory until one is dominant over the other, and the one gives up and flees.

Ephesians 6:12 states, *"For we wrestle not against flesh and blood, but against principalities, against powers, against the rulers of the darkness of this world, against spiritual wickedness in high places."* We must fight to be who God called us to be. We must fight to overcome the spirit of deception. We have dominion, so we will always be dominant over the devil. We must stop giving the devil access to our power and dominion. We are created in God's image to have dominion over *"every living thing that moveth upon the earth."* This includes the devil and all that are a part of his kingdom. James 4:7, *"Submit yourselves therefore to God. Resist the devil, and he will flee from you."* The roaring lion will always flee the bold lion because that boldness is through the power and dominion given to you by God. When the devil comes roaring, be that bold lion that speaks the word. The boldness only comes with the recognition of the problem that there is a CLOG.

Now you've seen that the water has come back up to the point of overflowing onto the floor. This means other things are being destroyed and damaged by this CLOG. There's this feeling of being lost, not knowing what to do. The water is cleaned up, but there's no fix to the problem. There's now recognition of a problem, but no readily available solution because the cause of the problem is not known. There's a realization that the problem still exists because it wasn't properly fixed the first time it occurred. Let's just use another sink. This is what happens when we have options. We won't go to God. We just call upon family, friends, doctor, pastor, anybody but God. Still not using that resource, still not getting that problem fixed. Closest sink to go use, but we rather walk to one that's a little further away because we know it's currently working.

Now, something has happened where the sink needs to be available. The water is gone, no visible signs of a problem, but it's a lingering feeling of knowing what's going to occur when the water is turned back on. Life is in a good place, things finally on track, learning lessons from repeated mistakes, and growing as a person, so it appears. Then all hell breaks loose. It's time to use the sink and the water is back. You get the help you need, but it's only a temporary fix. There's air now coming through the pipe, so the problem has become severe and most likely, costly.

Luke 14:27-35 makes it clear. *"And whosoever doth not bear his cross, and come after me, cannot be my disciple. 28 For which of you, intending to build a tower, sitteth not down first, and counteth the cost, whether he have sufficient to finish it? 29 Lest haply, after he hath laid the foundation, and is not able to finish it, all that behold it begin to mock him, 30 Saying, This man began to build, and was not able to finish. 31 Or what king, going to make war against another king, sitteth not down first, and consulteth whether he be able with ten thousand to meet him that cometh against him with twenty thousand? 32 Or else, while the other is yet a great way off, he sendeth an ambassage, and desireth conditions of peace. 33 So likewise, whosoever he be of you that forsaketh not all that he hath, he cannot be my disciple. 34 Salt is good: but if the salt have lost his savour, wherewith shall it be seasoned? 35 It is neither fit for the land, nor yet for the dunghill; but men cast it out. He that hath ears to hear, let him hear."*

Count the costs of not fixing that CLOG. What long term damage is being done? Whose blessing is being delayed by our lack of obedience? What manifested blessings are being delayed in our own lives? What prayers are being hindered because of this CLOG? Are you ready to be a disciple of God? God gave his disciples an assignment.

Mathew 28:16-20, *"Then the eleven disciples went away into Galilee, into a mountain where Jesus had appointed them. 17 And when they saw him, they worshipped him: but some doubted. 18 And Jesus came and spake unto them, saying, All power is given unto me in heaven and in earth. 19 Go ye therefore, and teach all nations, baptizing them in the name of the Father, and of the Son, and of the Holy Ghost: 20 Teaching them to observe all things whatsoever I have commanded you: and, lo, I am with you always, even unto the end of the world. Amen."* We can't be disciples for Christ if we have a CLOG. It's time to find the root cause of the problem and fix it. Stay with me because I'm going to continue to talk in parallels as we go further.

The way to find the root cause of a problem is analysis. We're going to have to examine some things and take some things apart to see what's causing the CLOG. We may think we know, but I found out in a project I just completed, that's it's not always what it may appear to be. A further and deeper analysis must be done. We know we've been deceived. How did we allow this spirit of deception to enter? What door was open to allow entrance into our lives? Why was deception allowed to enter? When did this deception take place? We know who deceived us and where we were deceived. We've allowed the spirit of deception to enter our lives causing us to deceive ourselves in our hearts and minds. We must now answer these other questions then take them a step further.

We allowed the spirit of deception to enter through our desires. Psalms 37:4 says, *"Delight thyself also in the LORD: and he shall give thee the desires of thine heart."* The critical part of that scripture that we look past is the beginning, *"Delight thyself also in the Lord."* We want to have the manifestations of our desires, but our desires didn't come from God if we didn't delight ourselves in Him. Ephesians 2:1-3, *"And you hath he quickened, who were dead in trespasses and sins; ² Wherein in time past ye walked according to the course of this world, according to the prince of the power of the air, the spirit that now worketh in the children of disobedience: ³ Among whom also we all had our conversation in times past in the lusts of our flesh, fulfilling the desires of the flesh and of the mind; and were by nature the children of wrath, even as others."* We were in sin fulfilling the desires of the flesh, and after we received salvation, we continued to fulfill the desires of our flesh.

We never cast out the spirit of deception; therefore, we are still being deceived. Paul says it this way in Romans 7:18-25, *"For I know that in me (that is, in my flesh,) dwelleth no good thing: for to will is present with me; but how to perform that which is good I find not .¹⁹ For the good that I would I do not: but the evil which I would not, that I do. ²⁰ Now if I do that I would not, it is no more I that do it, but sin that dwelleth in me. ²¹ I find then a law, that, when I would do good, evil is present with me. ²² For I delight in the law of God after the inward man: ²³ But I see another law in my members, warring against the law of my mind, and bringing me into captivity to the law of sin which is in my members. ²⁴ O wretched man that I am! who shall deliver me from the body of this death? ²⁵ I thank God through Jesus Christ our Lord. So then with the mind I myself serve the law of God; but with the flesh the law of sin."*

We're still going after the desires of our flesh instead of delighting in the Lord and getting those desires that are given by Him and manifested through Him. Our fleshly desires are strongholds. When I say fleshly desires, that's anything that is not of the will of God for our lives which we place above God. For example, a woman desires a husband. That's the will of God for her life, to have a husband. What makes it a fleshly desire is when she seeks after the husband, instead of him finding her, which is the word of God. *"Whoso findeth a wife findeth a good thing, and obtaineth favour of the LORD,"* Proverbs 18:22. What makes it a fleshly desire is when she loses patience for who God has for her and marries the first man that shows interest. What makes it a fleshly desire is when she turns away from God because things aren't happening according to her plans, in her time. She placed that desire above all else.

The Bible says in 2 Corinthians 10:3-6, *"For though we walk in the flesh, we do not war after the flesh: 4 (For the weapons of our warfare are not carnal, but mighty through God to the pulling down of strong holds;)5 Casting down imaginations, and every high thing that exalteth itself against the knowledge of God, and bringing into captivity every thought to the obedience of Christ; 6 And having in a readiness to revenge all disobedience, when your obedience is fulfilled."* We must get to a place of obedience and get the mind of Christ, so we pull down those fleshly desires and bring them into captivity. Philippians 2:5 says, *"Let this mind be in you, which was also in Christ Jesus:"*. 1 Corinthians 2:15-16 in the amplified says, *"But the spiritual man [the spiritually mature Christian] judges all things [questions, examines and applies what the Holy Spirit reveals], yet is himself judged by no one [the unbeliever cannot judge and understand the believer's spiritual nature]. 16 For WHO HAS KNOWN THE MIND and*

PURPOSES OF THE LORD, SO AS TO INSTRUCT HIM? *But we have the mind of Christ [to be guided by His thoughts and purposes]."* We are to be guided by God's thoughts and purposes. Delighting ourselves in Him will give us that guidance. The first part of that scripture says, *"But the spiritual man [the spiritually mature Christian] judges all things [questions, examines and applies what the Holy Spirit reveals],".* How can we question, examine, and apply what the Holy Spirit reveals if we have a CLOG where we can't even hear what the Holy Spirit is saying? Remember, we had other options where we didn't have to use that sink. We had other sinks that could be used, so that resource wasn't being used. We see the resource of the Holy Spirit, but we don't even recognize His voice because we haven't used that resource for a period. We were in disobedience and being deceived by our fleshly desires, as a result, we didn't heed the Holy Spirit's warnings and the spirit of deception was having her way.

How did the sink get a blockage? Still don't know. Must go further. Let's start taking some pipes apart to see what things went into the sink that could be the cause of the blockage. In the sink, there is a stopper where it allows the water to go out, but it should stop foreign particles from entering the pipes. Although there is a small opening for the water to drain, you've seen at times where other things go down the drain that could potentially cause a problem. What door in your life was there just a small enough opening to allow that spirit of deception to enter? The door was vulnerability. To be vulnerable is to be open to temptation, open to assault in a position that is difficult to defend. There was this desire, a longing in your life that you spoke with your mouth. When you spoke it, the devil heard it and there was the opening. The tongue is a powerful instrument. James 3:5-10 states, *"Even so the tongue is a little member, and boasteth great things. Behold, how great a matter a little fire kindleth! ⁶ And the tongue is a fire, a world of iniquity: so is the tongue among our members, that it defileth the whole body, and setteth on fire the course of nature; and it is set on fire of hell. ⁷ For every kind of beasts, and of birds, and of serpents, and of things in the sea, is tamed, and hath been tamed of mankind: ⁸ But the tongue can no man tame; it is an unruly evil, full of deadly poison. ⁹ Therewith bless we God, even the Father; and therewith curse we men, which are made after the similitude of God. ¹⁰ Out of the same mouth proceedeth blessing and cursing. My brethren, these things ought not so to be."*

Proverbs is full of verses concerning the tongue. 18:21, *"Death and life are in the power of the tongue: and they that love it shall eat the fruit thereof."* 21:23, *"Whoso keepeth his mouth and his tongue keepeth his soul from troubles."* 15:4, *"A wholesome tongue is a tree of life: but perverseness therein is a breach in the spirit."* The problem is not speaking it, but *when* we speak it. How is the heart and mind when we speak it? The Bible says in Luke 6:45, *"A good man out of the good treasure of his heart bringeth forth that which is good; and an evil man out of the evil treasure of his heart bringeth forth that which is evil: for of the abundance of the heart his mouth speaketh."* Do we speak of that desire when we're not delighting in the Lord? Do we speak that desire when we're frustrated with life? Do we speak that desire when we're heartbroken? Do we speak that desire when we're jealous and envious of others who have what we desire? Proverbs 4:23 says, *"Keep thy heart with all diligence; for out of it are the issues of life."* Do we speak it when we're full of anger, resentment, and unforgiveness? Do we speak it when we're full of unrepentance, disobedience, and unbelief? To clear that CLOG, we must get our hearts and minds right.

David said in Psalms 51:10, *"Create in me a clean heart, O God; and renew a right spirit within me."* Psalms 19:12-14, *"Who can understand his errors? cleanse thou me from secret faults.* *13 Keep back thy servant also from presumptuous sins; let them not have dominion over me: then shall I be upright, and I shall be innocent from the great transgression. 14 Let the words of my mouth, and the meditation of my heart, be acceptable in thy sight, O LORD, my strength, and my redeemer."* We must remove anything that is not like God out of our hearts and minds. James 4:8 in The Living Bible translation says, *"And when you draw close to God, God will draw close to you. Wash your hands, you sinners, and let your hearts be filled with God alone to make them pure and true to him."*

When we examine ourselves, we must rid ourselves of some things. Those hurts that we're holding onto, that shame we're still holding onto, that guilt we're still holding onto, that unforgiveness that we're holding onto, that pity and sorrow we're holding onto. Anything that can become a stronghold and opening for the devil. We must ask God to remove all of it, and fill us up with his goodness, his compassion, his word, his deeds, and his holiness. All things that are like and of Him. We must cast out that spirit of deception and allow the Holy Spirit to take over and take charge. Clean and clear those pipes out of all the crud that may cause another CLOG.

We must still discover why, so that it's not allowed to happen again. What made us vulnerable to the point that we could be made to deceive ourselves? Was it a lack of being or feeling loved, a lack of belonging, a feeling of unworthiness, a feeling of disappointment, or a feeling of loneliness? Only you know the truth. Search yourselves and be honest with yourselves. This is the way of preventing another CLOG. Once we're honest with ourselves, we must then apply the blood of Jesus to our hearts and minds as a covering, as a cleanser, as a disinfectant, and as a protectant.   The amplified version of Ephesians 1:7 says, *"In Him we have redemption [that is, our deliverance and salvation] through His blood, [which paid the penalty for our sin and resulted in] the forgiveness and complete pardon of our sin, in accordance with the riches of His grace..."* Colossians 1:20-22, *"And, having made peace through the blood of his cross, by him to reconcile all things unto himself; by him, I say, whether they be things in earth, or things in heaven. 21 And you, that were sometime alienated and enemies in your mind by wicked works, yet now hath he reconciled 22 In the body of his flesh through death, to present you holy and unblameable and unreproveable in his sight:".*

Titus 2:14 states, *"Who gave himself for us, that he might redeem us from all iniquity, and purify unto himself a peculiar people, zealous of good works."* We must have the faith to believe that we are redeemed, reconciled, pardoned through the power of His blood.   When we feel another door trying to crack open, we know to seal it with the blood of Jesus.

It's important to know when the door was open because it gives answers to other questions. With the sink, it was years ago when the blockage first occurred. What resource is lying dormant in your life? I put it out of my mind because I didn't have a need for it at the time. When I had a need for it, it wasn't available. Now there was this urgency to clean up the mess and get the problem fixed. Are there some urgent situations in your life where you need some prayers answered right away? Do you need a suddenly? Do you need God to show up right now? Most likely, it's not going to happen. The Holy Spirit has been living on the inside of us and we ignored him. We didn't heed his nudging, his warnings, his guidance, and his direction. Now we want from him a quick response because of situations that are urgent to us. He already knew we would be in those situations.

We want him to clean up our mess and fix the problem, only to create another mess and problem. When that door was opened all those years ago, a month ago, a week ago, what effect did it have on those around you, those in your life, on you? That spirit of deception may have caused some erosion of relationships or friendships, unbelievers not wanting anything to do with God, the disconnection of purposeful partnerships, my brothers to stumble, and so much more. However long ago it was that we were deceived, we must right our wrongs that happened during that time. Restoration, rebuilding, and renewing must take place. You may ask yourself why my prayers aren't being answered, why haven't things manifested yet, what am I not doing, what am I doing wrong? You don't get a response, at least you think you don't.

Here it is. Your response, your answer. Isaiah 58, our foundational text, covers the correct way to fast. Matthew 17:20-22 says, *"And Jesus said unto them, Because of your unbelief: for verily I say unto you, If ye have faith as a grain of mustard seed, ye shall say unto this mountain, Remove hence to yonder place; and it shall remove; and nothing shall be impossible unto you. 21 Howbeit this kind goeth not out but by prayer and fasting."* Some situations take more than just praying; some require fasting. To fast means to abstain from food or a limiting on one's food. Fasting is not just about food. Here is Isaiah 58:1-12 in the message translation, *"1-3 "Shout! A full-throated shout! Hold nothing back—a trumpet-blast shout! Tell my people what's wrong with their lives, face my family Jacob with their sins! They're busy, busy, busy at worship, and love studying all about* me. To all appearances they're a nation of right-living people—law-abiding, God-honoring. They ask me, 'What's the right thing to do?' and love having me on their side. But they also complain, 'Why do we fast and you don't look our way? Why do we humble ourselves and you don't even notice?' **3-5** "Well, here's why: "The bottom line on your 'fast days' is profit. You drive your employees much too hard. You fast, but at the same time you bicker and fight. You fast, but you swing a mean fist. The kind of fasting you do won't get your prayers off the ground. Do you think this is the kind of fast day I'm after: a day to show off humility? To put on a pious long face and parade around solemnly in black? Do you call that fasting, a fast day that I, GOD, would like? **6-9** "This is the kind of fast day I'm after: to break the chains of injustice, get rid of exploitation in the workplace, free the oppressed, cancel debts. What I'm interested in seeing you do is: sharing your food with the hungry, inviting the homeless poor into your homes, putting clothes on the shivering ill-clad, being available to your own families. Do this and the lights will turn on, and your lives will turn around at once. Your righteousness will pave your way. The GOD of glory will secure your passage. Then when you pray, GOD will answer. You'll call out for help and I'll say, 'Here I am.' **9-12** "If you get rid of unfair practices, quit blaming victims, quit gossiping about other people's sins, If you are generous with the hungry and start giving yourselves to the down-and-out, Your lives will begin to glow in the darkness, your shadowed lives will be bathed in sunlight. I will always show you where to go. I'll give you a full life in the emptiest of places— firm muscles, strong bones. You'll be like a well-watered garden, a gurgling spring that never runs dry. You'll use the old rubble of past lives to build anew, rebuild the foundations from out of your past. You'll be known as those who can fix anything, restore old ruins, rebuild and renovate, make the community livable again."

God tells us exactly what to fast for, exactly what to do to get our prayers answered. None of it is about us. He tells us when we do a proper fast for others, what he will make happen for us. If you've been fasting incorrectly or not at all, you now have that knowledge. When your prayers aren't being answered, then you know that you need to check yourself and check if you're praying correctly. If both are in line with the word, then we must take it to a higher level and fast. I began and ended with fasting because many of us don't fast, don't know how to fast, don't know why we fast, and only fast when it's called upon by service leadership (The Apostles, Bishops, Ministers, Pastors, and so forth). Hopefully, this lesson will start more of us to praying and fasting more, not for ourselves but for others. As you see in the last few verses, fasting can make that restoration, rebuilding, and renewing possible from past mistakes, from the past deception. Fasting is a preventive measure of not getting a CLOG. Fasting will give you boldness and confidence because you're in tune with the Spirit. The scripture says, *"You'll be known as those who can fix anything, restore old ruins, rebuild and renovate, make the community livable again."* In other words, you will be elevated.

Let's pray. I thank you Father that your word is going forth, and your people will have ears to hear, hearts to receive, and the wisdom of God in their minds to understand. I thank you Lord that we have no more CLOGs. We are removing the Constraining Limits on God. We know that all things are possible with God, and He is a limitless God. Nothing is too hard for God. Lord, I declare that your people's eyes are open to the spirit of deception, and they are casting that spirit out of their lives right now in the name of Jesus to never enter no more. I declare that they can see and know the truth. I ask that you remove anything from our lives that is unlike you. Lord, I ask that you cleanse us from all unrighteousness and forgive us our sins that we've committed knowingly and unknowingly. Lord, grant us the boldness needed to fulfill our purpose on the Earth. Let us speak the word of truth boldly without fear, reservation, or hesitation. Lord, we apply the blood of Jesus and your healing power to past hurts, past shames, past guilts and by your blood, we no longer feel that hurt, that shame, and that guilt. Thank you, Lord, for giving us back our dominion and power.

Satan, I serve you notice that you have no place in the lives of God's people. You must flee in the name of Jesus. You have no authority over us. We are overcomers and victorious through Jesus Christ. Lord, I thank you for the revelation of fasting. Because of this lesson, I know more people will begin to fast and fast according to your word. I pray that more people become disciples to be used by You, so they can spread the gospel of Jesus Christ and His grace. As we move forward, I thank you and praise you in advance for more revelation, knowledge, more wisdom, more spiritual growth, and more people coming into the knowledge of You and entering your kingdom through salvation. In Jesus' Name, amen.

Moving Beyond the Pain
God's Will vs. The Flesh

Foundational texts:

Lamentations 1:2 *She weepeth sore in the night, and her tears are on her cheeks: among all her lovers she hath none to comfort her: all her friends have dealt treacherously with her, they are come her enemies.*

Jeremiah 3:1 *They say, if a man put away his wife, and she go from him, and become another man's, shall he return unto her again? Shall not that land be greatly polluted? but thou has played the harlot with many lovers; yet return again to me, saith the Lord.*

The foundational texts refer to Jerusalem and Israel, but I thought to use them to apply to my relationships. We've all faced painful situations in life such as a broken heart, the loss of a loved one, a friendship ending, losing a job, and many others. There is a saying that time heals all wounds. I believe that time helps, but there is only one thing that heals, the love of God. When you have a relationship with God and truly love Him, and allow Him to love you, you're able to forgive, to love and trust again, and have faith in yourself and others. I was once deeply hurt, and as a result, I spiraled out of control.

I made some choices that I shouldn't have made, which delayed many blessings for my life. While I was making all these unrighteous choices, I still attended church. I actually attended church more. I would go to Bible study, seminars, and buy different tapes, books, and CDs from different ministries.

Throughout my unrighteousness, God was still there for me and was still working on me to get me back on the right path. Thank God for his grace and mercy. We had been friends since the third grade and neither one of us wanted the friendship to end because the relationship hadn't worked out. I was able to maintain a friendship with the person that I allowed to hurt me, but the friendship was different. Now I said allowed to hurt me because I control, and you control, what you let another person do to you. It wasn't easy to keep the friendship. I was reminded daily of the choices he made and that kept the pain at the forefront. I finally just buried the pain. When you bury the pain, you haven't really faced it and allowed the love of God to heal you of the pain. When God heals you of the pain, you can look back on the situation and not feel any pain. You will have the memory, but there is no longer any pain associated with the memory. You're even able to talk about the situation without feeling any pain or getting emotional.

We both moved on with our lives, but our hearts were still intertwined. The love we had for one another was never lost. Some years had passed, and he wrote me a letter expressing how he felt. I read the letter and put it away. I said to myself, he hurt me too bad, and I wasn't going to put myself through that again. I never responded to his letter. A few years passed, and here he was trying again. Thank God for his determination. He would always express himself and his feelings. I would hear him, my heart would hear him, but I just wasn't willing to take the chance. All I could think about was the pain and how I was hurt before. I had always said to myself that I wasn't going back to anyone. I considered it moving backwards. God's plan isn't always what we have planned or want for ourselves. It came to a point where I was talking to him all the time, all throughout the day, almost every day. I was beginning to feel something again, but I wasn't going to let him know it. I still wasn't willing to take a chance. Well one day, I was talking to God and telling Him I was ready for a relationship. He answered. When he answered, I said, you're kidding me right. You can't be serious. Not him. No way. God showed me the face of my friend. When you ask God for something, be ready for the answer.

God never said that this life would be easy. He never said that there wouldn't be pain, trials, tribulations, sorrows, and tests. In I Corinthians 10:13, it says, *"There hath no temptation taken you but such as is common to man: but God is faithful, who will not suffer you to be tempted above that ye are able; but will with the temptation also make a way to escape, that ye may be able to bear it."* Many times we bring the pain and sorrow, the trials and tribulations upon ourselves because we are following our wills and the lust of the flesh and not following the will of God. This is true for me. I made decisions to do what I wanted to do when I wanted to do it. The flesh was reigning in my life. Romans 7:18 says, *"For I know that in me (that is, in my flesh,) dwelleth no good thing: for to will is present with me; but how to perform that which is good I find not."*

When I was living in sin, I knew what I was doing was wrong. When you're saved and your spirit man becomes alive to God, the Holy Spirit talks to you. Just think about situations that you've been in before and you knew you shouldn't have been where you were at, and you hear the voice telling you don't do it; you see your way of escape and you don't take it. You're making a conscious decision to commit that sin. The Bible says in Romans 6:23, *"For the wages of sin is death; but the gift of God is eternal life through Jesus Christ our Lord."* When we're living in the flesh and committing fleshly sins, it may feel good at the time, but the feeling doesn't last. Think about how you felt when it was over. When you've committed an evil act, did you really feel good once it was done, or did you instantly have regrets? Think about the long-term effects, something is dying when we sin. For me, I still felt depressed and was really miserable, living a life full of regrets, wishing I could have a do over; I was dying on the inside. I was searching for something that I knew I could only find in God. God will allow things to continue happening, but He has a way to get your attention. Well, he got my attention.

I talked about the flesh and sin because it's a large part of the pain. When we feel emotional pain, we tend to turn to the flesh to lessen the hurt of the pain, but in actuality, we're only causing more hurt and pain for ourselves but in different ways. I went to the doctor for my regular checkup, and the results were not in my favor. Thank God that it wasn't anything serious, but what it said to me is that I needed to make a change before something serious happened. God was giving me a chance to repent, ask for forgiveness, and turn back to Him. Guess what, I did. It was a struggle. Matthew 26:41 says, *"Watch and pray, that ye enter not into temptation: the spirit indeed is willing, but the flesh is weak."* When the flesh would attempt to make itself known, I would start listening to my gospel music and calling on the name of Jesus. It works. I was able to get past that moment, claim victory, and move on.

After becoming consistent with turning to Him and His word when temptation was at hand, it became easier and the temptations less frequent. James 4:7 tells you how to overcome the flesh. It says, *"Submit yourselves therefore to God. Resist the devil, and he will flee from you."* Until you're ready to surrender your will to God's will, the flesh will continue to have the victory. You move beyond the pain caused by the flesh by consistently walking in His word and in His will. It may take some time, but as you continually walk with God and grow a stronger relationship with Him, you reach a point where you can forgive yourself for past mistakes. God has already forgiven us, so we must learn to forgive ourselves. We have to have faith in God and trust that He knows who and what is best for our lives. He created us for his works and knows what will fulfill us. Hebrews 10:22-23 says, *"Let us draw near with a true heart in full assurance of faith, having our hearts sprinkled from an evil conscience, and our bodies washed with pure water. Let us hold fast the profession of our faith without wavering: (for he is faithful that promised:)."* You will not be fulfilled until you're doing the will of God. You will always feel like something is missing and never be truly satisfied with your life.

Like I stated previously, when I heard and saw God's answer about a relationship, I wasn't feeling it at all. It took a little while to digest. When I received God's answer, I did a complete one eighty. There's a difference. When you only hear what God has to say, you take no action. When you receive what God says, action follows. I completely embraced the idea of the relationship and made some changes in my thinking. Believe me when I say, God had to work on my way of thinking, and I'm still a work in progress. Before God had answered my request, we had been communicating, and we were able to discuss the mistakes, hurt, and pain of the past that was caused by one another. Talking is very therapeutic. I was able to understand his point of view and decisions, and he was able to understand my point of view and decisions. Of course, we didn't agree with them, but we had that understanding. We had also maintained a level of respect for one another. There was never any physical or verbal abuse. Neither of us was cussing one another, calling each other any derogatory name, or talking down to one another. If you have that going on in your relationship, you need to stop it now and examine why you're doing it. To this day, we still don't. Just by having those conversations, the pain and hurt had decreased. It wasn't completely gone, but the elephant was no longer in the room. During that digestion period when I heard and saw God's answer, I told God he was going to have to help me move beyond the pain for this relationship this to work. This is what God did in my situation. God showed himself in my friend. That was all it took for me. I received God's answer and it was so unbelievable to me how once I received his answer, the pain was gone and my heart was filled with so much love. All of the feelings came rushing back, and they were actually stronger than before. When God has his hands on your relationship, every situation and circumstance can be overcome.

Now the devil knows the power the two of you have together, so brace yourself for the tests. He will throw everything at you. Ephesians 6:11 says, *"Put on the whole armor of God, that ye may be able to stand against the wiles of the devil."* I have to be honest and say we failed many times at the beginning. First, was the lust of the flesh. We were defeated, but not for long. We both had been living holy lives and wanted to continue to please God in that area, so we made a joint decision to abstain from lusts of the flesh. I Peter 2:11 says, *"Dearly beloved, I beseech you as strangers and pilgrims, abstain from fleshly lusts, which war against the soul:"*. In I Thessalonians 4:3-4, 7, it says, *"For this is the will of God, even your sanctification, that ye should abstain from fornication: that every one of you should know how to possess his vessel in sanctification and honor...For God hath not called us unto uncleanness, but unto holiness."*

Next, was Satan's use of fiery darts. Fiery darts are thoughts that are contrary to the will of God. He was having thoughts of unworthiness, infidelity, and abandonment. I was having thoughts about reliving the past, not being a priority in his life, and the relationship just not working. This was another victory for Satan, but not for long. We didn't share how we were feeling with another until we were both hurt and upset. We talked about how we felt and reassured one another of our commitment to each other. We also prayed that what we were feeling would be taken away from us and that we would be delivered from having doubts. No more doubts. Now when we have contrary thoughts, we give no place or voice to them. We recognize who it is and what he's attempting to do, and we don't allow him into the relationship. If we feel that one is wrong, we allow the Holy Spirit to correct us, and we're both good at admitting when we're wrong. Once Satan realized that he could no longer defeat us in that area, he moved to two of his major weapons: the weapon of fear on him and the weapon of frustration on me.

Once again, we were defeated, but not for long. Through the lack of communication, we allowed Satan to defeat us. We separated in a sense that we allowed God to work on us individually, so he could focus on what he needed to do to pay a vow to God and overcome his fear, and so I could overcome my frustration. I was able to overcome my frustration through the Word. I had slacked off on listening to my gospel music and being in the Word. Once I got back on track, I was no longer frustrated. Paul said to the Philippian church in Philippians 4:11, *"Not that I speak in respect of want: for I have learned, in whatsoever state I am, therewith to be content".* I started claiming peace and contentment for my life and that's what I received. Things that were bothering me no longer bothered me; things that I allowed to anger and upset me, no longer had that effect on me. Hebrews 11:6 says, *"But without faith it is impossible to please him: for he that cometh to God must believe that he is, and that he is a rewarder of them that diligently seek him."* When you seek God, he will reward you.

I've received a great reward for seeking God and submitting to His will. I have the man in my life that was designed and created for me. He truly loves me with his body, soul, and spirit. He treats me like the queen that I am. He truly loves and serves God with all of himself. He keeps God first, and as a result, he is blessed beyond measure. Matthew 6:33 says, *"But seek ye first the kingdom of God, and his righteousness; and all these things shall be added unto you."* When you look at him from a worldly view or man's standpoint, you may think that he doesn't have much, but if you hear his testimonies on how he got what he has, you will realize that he has more than most of us.

This world will pass away and the things that we see are temporary. 2 Corinthians 4:18 says, *"While we look not at the things which are seen, but at the things which are not seen: for the things which are seen are temporal; but the things which are not seen are eternal."* We can't take it with us. What counts the most is our spiritual blessings. When you look at him from a spiritual standpoint, he is filthy rich. His level of spiritual richness is what makes me love him the more. It's what matters to me. What he has to offer me is more important than the material things in this world. He lifts my spirit. He gives me words of wisdom. He ministers to my soul. He keeps me balanced. He covers me with his prayers. He makes me laugh and smile all of the time. He makes me feel loved.

To get to this point, it took time and patience. You have to be open and vulnerable. You have to be willing to go through the process, and it is a process. We want a quick fix when everything can't be done quickly. You must be willing to put your heart in God's hands and trust that he will take care of it. Don't lean unto your own understanding but acknowledge God in all your ways and he shall direct your path. You must allow God to order your steps. If you claimed him as Lord of life, you must let him be Lord of your life and submit to His will. I found that life is better after I moved out of my way.